The Stories That Haunt Us

Bill Jessome

NIMBUS
PUBLISHING

For Heather Proudfoot

Nimbus Publishing Limited
PO Box 9166
Halifax, NS   B3K 5M8
(902) 455-4286

Printed and bound in Canada
Design: Margaret Issenman

Library and Archives Canada Cataloguing in Publication
Jessome, Bill
The stories that haunt us / Bill Jessome.
ISBN 1-55109-483-5

1. Ghosts—Maritime Provinces. 2. Tales—Maritime Provinces. 3. Ghost stories, Canadian—Maritime Provinces. I. Title.

GR113.5.M37J474 2004   398.2'0971505   C2004-905674-3

We acknowledge the financial support of the Government of Canada through the Book Publishing Industry Development Program (BPIDP) and the Canada Council for our publishing activities.

Table of Contents

Besides this earth, and besides the race of men,
there is an invisible world and a kingdom of
spirits; that world is round us, for it is everywhere...
—Charlotte Brontë, *Jane Eyre*

Introduction

Yes, I know I went out on a limb and told you devotees of the paranormal that there were no more ghostly tales worth telling. How wrong I was! Ghost stories are endless and ever-changing. They've been around forever—why, these wandering souls have been here since before the written word, for this is the stuff of the great storytellers. And yes, gentle hearts, such stories are as old still as the first human to slip into the abyss. Does that mean each of us carries our own ghost within, which will rise when we are no more? How perceptive you are, dear reader. How very perceptive indeed. Please read on…

Chapter One

Roadside Spectres

The Woebegone Ghost

It was late evening but not yet dark when Ethan Carmichael encountered the lone man on the side of the road. Ethan thought the man might be someone he knew, but when he got a closer look at the man's face he didn't recognize him. Ethan got down from his wagon and stood a couple of feet from the stranger. It was then he realized this was no man at all—he was looking right through him! The ghost was sitting on a large tree stump, and Ethan could see straight through him.

Not a man easily scared, Ethan spoke to the apparition. "Good evening to you, sir. My name is Ethan Carmichael. Something I can do for you?" The ghost told Ethan his name was Hector Piercey and explained that his spirit could not rest until he found his body and saw that it was given a Christian burial. Ethan asked where Hector's physical body was located. The ghost replied, "A place called the Thistle farm. It used to be located just across the way, but now it's gone. I'm certain this is where it was. That's why I was sitting here wondering what to do. I cannot rest until I find my body."

"Well," said Ethan, "I've been living in these parts for a long time and I've never heard of the Thistle farm." It was obvious by the expression on the ghost's face that he was confused and frustrated. Without a word, and in obvious despair, the ghost let out a wail and disappeared.

When Ethan got home he told his wife Susan about his experience with the ghost. She cocked her head to one side and smiled at her husband. "You had a few in town, I suspect. The ghost is more likely the spirits in your belly, I'd say."

Ethan persevered and told her the story. "The poor soul lost his body and now he's upset and confused because the place where he said it was hidden, the Thistle farm, is no longer there. I told him that for as long as I've lived around these parts, there was never a place known as the Thistle farm. Anyway, I'll be back there tomorrow evening at the same time to see if I can help the poor man. I'm told ghosts appear mostly in the same place."

True to his word, Ethan was back the next day at the same time. Sitting on the same tree stump was the ghost. Ethan stopped the horse but didn't get down from the buckboard immediately. For a few minutes they stared at each other. This time, though, Ethan noticed something different about the ghost's demeanour. He wore an expression of deep sadness—it seemed as though he might burst into tears at any moment. Ethan got down, and this time he sat on the tree stump next to the ghost.

"So," Ethan said. "Tell me the problem and we'll see if we can come up with a solution for you." The ghost nodded. He then pulled down his shirt collar revealing an ugly circular scar on his neck. It was an obvious sign that he met his death on the gallows.

"You were hanged?"

The ghost nodded.

"What happened?"

So the ghost of Hector Piercey told Ethan the sad tale of his demise:

I was passing through here on my way to the city when night came. I didn't have any money for lodgings, so I just slept in a barn loft at the Thistle farm, not wanting to impose on anyone, you see. But sometime before dawn, half a dozen men dragged me out of the loft and before I had a chance to explain myself or ask why they were so angry, I found myself strung up on a tree! Then, just before everything went dark, I heard one of those men say, 'That's one less horse thief to worry about.'

"I tried to scream at them, 'I'm no horse thief!' But I suddenly realized that I was sitting on the edge of the hayloft, looking down at the men. They were digging a shallow grave for my body. For a moment,

I couldn't understand how I could be in two places at the same time, sitting up there watching and at the same time hanging from a rope just outside. And then it hit me. I was a ghost! When the grave was deep enough I watched as one of the men went outside and loosened the rope. My body made a thumping sound when it hit the ground, and again when they brought me into the barn and dumped me into the shallow grave.

"After the last shovel of dirt was thrown on my grave, one of the men said, 'Who's ever going to know?' Then they uncorked a bottle and drank, swearing an oath to each other to never tell another soul about my murder.

"And now here I am on this tree stump. I think my soul has been in limbo, and the only thing I can figure out is that I need to find my remains and be buried in my family plot."

Ethan told Hector he would check with local historians and officials for a record of the Thistle farm first thing in the morning. He bid the poor ghost goodnight and returned home.

The next morning, Ethan was in the Registry of Deeds office minutes after it opened, asking about the farm Hector was hanged and buried on. "Yes," said the clerk. "The location you gave me is where the Thistle farm once stood. Following the death of its owner, however, the children allowed the farm to go to seed and it wasn't long before they abandoned the place. Vandals eventually burned down the buildings."

With this news, Ethan hurried back to the big tree stump. With a shovel slung over his shoulder and the ghost of Hector Piercey at his side, he made his way through the thick grass and in no time at all located the foundations of the house and barn. The shape of the foundation indicated where the entrance was, and from there Ethan and Hector measured the distance to the middle of the barn where Hector's body was buried.

Ethan drove the shovel into the ground, and just ten minutes later, he found what he had been looking for. He carefully lifted the skeletal remains of Hector Piercey and placed them gently in the box he had brought. He looked around for Hector, but the ghost was gone. Ethan knew, then, that he was gone for good.

Two days later, the remains of Hector Piercey were laid to rest in the family plot, with descendants of his family attending. There was a memorial following the burial, and one senior family member sought out Ethan.

"How well did you know our great-granduncle?'

"Not well at all, actually," Ethan replied.

The man wanted to know how Ethan had become involved in finding the remains. Rather than explaining his experience to the family, he simply said he had been hiking when he stumbled upon the remains. Erosion had worn away the shallow grave.

"Imagine our surprise, someone finding that murderous wretch after all these years!"

Ethan stared at the relative. "Murderous?"

"Oh, yes. Uncle Henry was convicted of murdering a local merchant but escaped the hangman's noose by overpowering the guards and escaping into the night, never to be seen or heard of again. They say he was a quite a convincing son of a gun."

Hocus-Pocus

*I*f he could help it, Doctor Neville Cross never refused a house call. It didn't matter what time of day or night it was, he would never put a patient off with "take two aspirin and call me in the morning." He travelled the back roads of the Maritimes in his black 1946 Pontiac Coupe to be at his patients' bedsides.

This was the case late one afternoon when the good doctor received an emergency call from Hector Mummery. Hector's wife, Zelda, was very ill and asked the doctor to come immediately. Some say Zelda Mummery was a hundred if she was a day. It was difficult to tell since her spine doubled her over and she rarely looked higher than one's kneecap because of excruciating pain. People living on or near the top of the mountain where Zelda lived avoided her because they believed she was a witch and that if they crossed her she'd put a hex on them.

Doctor Cross made his way to the Mummery house. Just as his car reached the top of Franey Mountain in Cape Breton, the rear right tire blew and he was forced off the road. He managed to change the blown tire and was lowering the car when suddenly it gave way, and came crashing down on his right shoulder. Pinned by the full weight of the car, Doctor Cross struggled to free himself. Darkness was quickly descending and the chill of the night air was settling into his bones. The doctor lay there looking skyward, cursing the clouds passing overhead that blocked out the moon.

With hope and life draining from him, Doctor Cross became aware of a splashing sound. It sounded as if someone was walking through the nearby puddles, making their way toward him. "Is someone there?" he called out. There was no response, just the sounds coming closer. Suddenly, the vehicle was lifted off his shoulder. Doctor Cross rolled out from under the clutches of the car and gingerly stood up. He checked his shoulder and was relieved to find it wasn't broken. He looked around to thank the person who had come to his aid, but there was no one. He heard nothing, saw nothing. Puzzled, the doctor got into his vehicle and hurried to the Mummerys'.

Doctor Cross knew what Zelda Mummery's medical problem was but she would not go to the hospital; she preferred, instead, to rely on her own remedies.

"You have cancer, Zelda, and you have no choice but to go to a hospital for proper treatment and care."

"No my potions will work. I just have to change the mix. Make em' stronger."

"You need to go to a hospital."

"I'll think about it," she said finally. But the doctor was firm with the old woman. "You take one of these tablets every four hours and none of that hocus pocus magic of yours."

The old woman looked at the doctor blankly, then beckoned him to lean in closer. He bent down and she whispered in his ear: "If it wasn't for my hocus pocus, you'd still be trapped under your car, dear doctor."

The Ghosts of Old Zeke and Molly Hill

When I began researching stories for this book, I was told that a hotbed for ghosts and mysteries was Pubnico, Nova Scotia, and that there would also be an amazing number of fascinating storytellers there. My friend was right—I found an abundance of both.

The storyteller of this tale is Laurent d'Entremont, who has generously allowed me to include in my book his encounter with the ghosts of old Zeke and Molly Hill. Laurent's true ghost story appeared in the *Yarmouth Vanguard* on October 29, 1991:

It was in the fall of the year, when the frost was on the pumpkin, and the corn was in the shock. The geese honking above were announcing their departure, and like many geese, I was on my way to River Bridge, New Brunswick, to visit my sister, Olive, and her family. River Bridge is close to the Nova Scotia border and received its name from the lone covered bridge over the narrow but swift Avonlea river.

Being one who enjoys the great outdoors, I kept an eye out for birds and waterfowl close to the road, with a little luck of maybe seeing a deer or two. What really caught my attention, though, was in late afternoon, when I was about 20 miles from my destination, a Model A Ford roadster was stopped by the side of the road and had its hood opened. An old-timer in farmer's overalls was working on the engine. The car was over-heating because of a faulty fan belt, a common thing in the early days of motoring.

He introduced himself as Zeke Hill. His wife, Molly, was inside the car knitting what looked like a heavy pair of fishermen mittens.

Zeke spoke fondly about his car. "This is the only car I ever had. I bought her new in 1930 and kept her all these years. Like me she is getting up there, but ain't over the hill yet. Tomorrow old man Lovitt over in River Bridge will fix my leaky water pump and install a new fan belt. Be good as new again."

A man who had kept the same car for over 40 years would make a pretty good story, I thought, as I parted company with old Zeke. The car had cooled down by then and roadside repairs would enable him to reach home.

Later, in River Bridge, I told my sister of my encounter with the Hills. She had never heard of Zeke or Molly Hill, but thought perhaps her husband Leonard knew them. He was away in Carraquet on business and would only be back the next day. Of course everybody knew old man Lovitt, who was quite the local character. Of my sister's three boys, Joseph, Lucien and François, it was François, the youngest, who shared my interest in old cars. He insisted that we visit Lovitt's garage in the morning.

We found old man Lovitt fiddling on some old relics of the past. The garage door was open, Lovitt was tall, straight as a rake handle and proud. The only thing which betrayed his age of four score plus one or two was his face, which was as weather beaten as the banks of the Petitcodiac.

"I understand that you have been running this place for 50 years" I ventured. "Yep, closer to 60." He was quite willing to talk, like most people of his age. "My brother Caleb and I, we built this place during the hungry twenties, we did all the work just the two of us."

Detecting my French accent, he asked where I was from. "West Pubnico," I told him. "I've been there once," he said. "Martha and me, we toured Nova Scotia about 20 years ago. We stayed overnight in Pubnico. Nice place."

But when I asked him at what time Zeke Hill was coming over with his Model A, an expression came on his face as if he had just seen a ghost. His answer was a real shocker, "Zeke Hill ain't coming here or going anywhere else, he's been dead for 25 years." "But I was talking with him yesterday," I insisted.

"Someone has been playing a trick on you" he said, then he told me the story of Zeke Hill.

Zeke and Molly Hill lived on a small farm about two miles from town. They made a meagre living out of farming and Molly sold woolen mittens to the local fishermen.

They bought only one car, a Ford Model A, which they kept for many, many years. One day in late fall, Zeke was coming from town when a young boy on a bicycle drove right into his path. He swerved to avoid hitting the boy, lost control of the car and went over the bank into the river close to the bridge. He died in the accident. Molly moved away after that and died a few years later. Now the farm was abandoned and the buildings were falling apart.

Since a man who had been dead for 25 years was not likely to show up (again), I changed the subject and asked if he had any car parts left over from the early days. He looked around, all he could find was a Model A fan belt. "Here take it," he said "I'll never use it now."

As we left, François asked me if I had seen the tag attached to the fan belt. I had. My heart almost stopped when I read "for Zeke Hill" written on the tag.

We decided to take a run over to visit the abandoned farm as François knew where it was. Devoid of life for a long time, the farm was a lonely place: one of the barn doors was off its hinges, swallows had made their nests on the rafters for years and a blue sky could be seen through holes in the roof. François suggested that we leave the old fan belt there, "for the ghost of Zeke Hill" —after all, it did belong to him. I went along with it. We left the belt hanging on a wooden peg near the door.

I went back home in West Pubnico and more or less forget all about it. No one would believe me anyway. But the ghost of Zeke Hill was not through yet. The next spring I received a phone call from New Brunswick. It was my nephew François. He was excited and talking at about 200 miles a minute. He slowed down enough so that I could get the gist of what he was saying.

A few days after I had left River Bridge, François and a friend took a bicycle trip to the old farm and, much to their surprise, the fan belt had vanished from where we had left it.

He said there was more. Recently a construction crew working on the road had dug up the remains of an old car near the bridge. Old man Lovitt had identified it as Zeke Hill's car. There wasn't much of the car left, most everything was rusted or gone, except the fan belt, which appeared to be brand new.

The Ghost Road

The salesman slowed his car as he came around the sharp curve, then picked up speed to begin the long, steep climb up the mountain. Suddenly, he saw something up ahead.

In the middle of the road a man, a woman, and a child stood waving. The man was waving a lantern from side to side. Thoughts of what he should do filled the salesman's mind. *Should I stop to help? Or should I just ignore them and not become involved? After all, they're strangers, and maybe the man uses the woman and child as a ploy to get unsuspecting strangers to stop. But how can I be so heartless as to refuse to help a mother and child in need?* He came to a stop and watched warily as the family moved to his side of the car.

To be on the safe side, the man kept the doors locked, but lowered his window just enough to speak to the father. The father smiled weakly.

"We didn't make that sharp turn back there. The car is at the bottom of the river. We were lucky to get out alive. We were on our way home. I guess we were a little too anxious to be back after being away for so long. We live just over the mountain about five miles from here. If you could give us a lift it would be much appreciated."

"Yes of course, please get in."

The mother and child said nothing. The man noted that they were completely expressionless. It was as if they were in a stupor. *Well, of course,* he thought. *They're still in shock.* The father on the other hand, was a talker. It took no time for the salesman to learn that the man had been born and raised on the mountain, and that he was a successful lumber mill operator and farmer. When they reached the farm gate, the salesman noticed a "for sale" sign nailed to the gate. He apologized but refused the man's invitation to stay overnight, telling him he had pressing matters to deal with.

Three days later the salesman was on the same road, driving the opposite way back to the city. When he reached the top of the mountain he stopped. He couldn't believe what he saw below him. Standing in the middle of the road was the family he had helped just days before. The father was waving a lantern from side to side, and on either side of him stood a woman and a child. It was then he understood. The family never did get out of the car when it went over the bank.

He pressed down on the gas and passed straight through the apparitions.

Chapter Two

One More Haunted House

The Ghost of the Five Fishermen

*A*h, historic Halifax, Nova Scotia—so full of history, so full of ghostly tales.

Stroll along Argyle Street to the World Trade Convention Centre, part of today's Halifax. Now take just a few steps more, and stop at the corner of Argyle and Carmichael streets. Here's where these ghostly tales begin.

First, a little history of the building itself. It was built in the early 1800s, when the Church of England decided the children of the poor needed a free education—with an emphasis on religion, of course. Anglican church members built a school on the corner of Argyle and Carmichael streets. To this day, you can see the pride that went into the construction of the building. The wall panelling is still rich and dark. Everything was built to last…and it has.

The school was such a success that eventually the building became too small for its purpose, so the school moved to bigger and better facilities and the building was sold to Anna Leonowens, who started a Victorian school of art. She was the governess to the King of Siam's children and her great adventure became a famous Broadway play and movie, *The King and I*. Eventually, Anna Leonowens had the same problem the church had: lack of space. She moved the art school to a larger facility. The building has changed hands quite a few time, but since the seventies, it has been home to the famous Five Fishermen restaurant.

I spent some time in the restaurant, getting a feel for the place. Leonard Currie, a senior staffer with a ghost story to share, tells me the spirit he came into contact with was very tall and mean.

"I was here alone one night, cleaning up, when I heard something fall to the floor. I went into the restaurant area to investigate and saw an ashtray on the floor. Remember, I was alone and the only way that ashtray could have ended up on the floor was if someone threw it there. Now, there was a mirror just above the table the ashtray would have been on, and when I was putting the ashtray back, I saw in that mirror the image of a stranger just over my shoulder, looking at me. He didn't move. He just stood there staring at me. Then he vanished, but not before I got a good look at him. The clothes he wore, including a long black coat, were definitely from another period."

Currie recalls other incidents when glassware and utensils were suddenly airborne. One time, just before closing, the only two employees in the restaurant heard a heated argument between two men in another part of the restaurant. When they went to investigate, the arguing stopped abruptly and the room was empty. Leonard Currie also says that staff will often be busily working when a rush of cold air passes over them, as though someone has just walked quickly by.

Leonard recalls the time an elderly lady came into the restaurant and a waiter seated her by the window facing Argyle Street. A short time later, the woman told him she couldn't stay. He said he'd find her another table. "No," the woman said, "It's the room. I just can't stay in it." She left.

That's not all Leonard Currie recalls. There was the time a waitress was standing by the salad bar when she suddenly felt a terrible pressure on her face, and there was nothing she could do to free herself from it. Whatever was pushing against her finally stopped, but it left a red mark on her cheek for days. And there have been numerous times when staff members have heard their names being called over and over again. They investigate and find nothing.

The staff goes about their business with fingers crossed and a prayer on their lips, hoping the ghosts don't bother them or their customers. It's speculation, of course, but some believe these wandering souls may be victims of the Halifax Explosion or the sinking of the *Titanic*. The bodies of many of the victims of these tragedies were brought to Snow's Funeral Home when the company occupied the building.

So the next time you and your lady or gentlemen friend are planning an evening on the town, the Five Fishermen restaurant is a great place to dine—so long as you keep a wary eye on who's watching you. If it's a tall gentleman with a long black coat and a scowl on his face, pay him no mind—unless he comes to your table!

The Dollhouse

I met an elderly lady during a book signing and she had a ghost story she wanted me to hear. It happened to a friend of her grandmother, Mrs. Flora Campbell. The house this friend lived in was haunted—or at least, the dollhouse in the house was haunted.

The owner of the house, which was in Annapolis Royal, was going overseas for three years to work as a missionary and asked Mrs. Campbell to house-sit her plants and two cats until she returned. Mrs. Campbell agreed and moved in. On the day of her departure, the owner delivered this ominous warning: "In a room on the third floor there is a dollhouse. It's locked and must remain so until I return. Under no circumstances should you or any of your friends enter this room. There is no reason for you to go inside and I implore you not to let curiosity get the best of you. Agreed?" Scared but too far in to turn back, Mrs. Campbell agreed.

It wasn't long, however, before the woman realized there was something not right—something disturbing—about the house. Late at night, the sounds of footsteps would awaken her from a sound sleep. She also heard mysterious giggling, like the laughter of naughty children. As soon as she'd get out of bed to investigate, she'd hear the scurrying of feet, then silence. After checking all the rooms on the second floor where she slept, she'd stand at the bottom of the stairs leading up to the third floor where the dollhouse was located, and listen. She knew she was being ridiculous but her curiosity took her up the stairs towards the forbidden room. She walked down the narrow hallway and stopped at the locked door, listening. It was distant and faint but she was sure she heard whispering. Shaking her head she went back to her room.

The next morning, while dusting a mantle clock, Mrs. Campbell accidentally flipped open the back panel. When she turned the clock around to snap the panel back in place, she couldn't help but notice a piece of bright red ribbon rolled-up inside. She took out the ribbon, and found a key attached. She knew instinctively that it was the key to the dollhouse. In her excitement and wonder, she forgot—or chose to forget—her promise to the owner. The only thing on her mind was discovering once and for all what was going on behind the locked door. When she got to the third floor, again she stopped and pressed her right ear against the door. Nothing. *A good sign*, she thought. Slowly, with a shaking hand, she inserted the key in the lock, turned it and opened the door. She flipped on the light switch and took in the contents of the room.

Mrs. Campbell couldn't believe the number of dolls! She counted 125 dolls lined up on shelves, chairs, the two windowsills, and the large bed. The woman wondered why anyone would lock up a room full of dolls as though they were dangerous, and began to walk around the room to get a closer look at the dolls' faces. The dolls were all shapes and sizes—one was even as big as a six-year-old child. She began to relax and enjoy looking at the dolls, when suddenly, in her periphery, something moved. Mrs. Campbell realized she had made a terrible mistake.

The missionary who owned the home became concerned when the letters stopped arriving from her friend. She telephoned the house, but there was no answer. She notified the police. The chief dispatched four policemen to investigate. The smallest officer slipped through a jimmied window and opened the front door for the other three.

There was no response to their calls so they went upstairs to look around. When nothing unusual was found on the second floor the police officers went up to the third floor. They noticed a locked door down the hall and one officer thought he heard whispering coming from the room. They decided to pick the lock, and the senior officer entered the room full of dolls. He started when he saw the body of Mrs. Campbell lying on the bed. She was dead. Several dolls knelt beside her on the bed, while others knelt on the floor. Lying next to the woman was a very large doll, about the size of young child, with its arms around the dead woman's neck.

As an aside, I will tell you of my own experience with strange and mysterious happenings. Dolls upset me. They sit there with that fixed stare and no matter how hard I try, I can't get rid of the feeling they're watching me.

A few years ago, while visiting a museum, I wandered off from my friends and ended up in a dark room that had a damp, musty odour. When my eyes adjusted to the darkness, I observed that everything in the room was black. On a black table in the centre of the room, with a large black bow around its middle, there was a long, narrow basket. I wondered what it was used for and later found out it was a death basket. Women's clothes, including a black dress, coat and hat, were draped over the end of a chair. On the floor in front of the chair was a pair of high button shoes. When I saw what was sitting on the shelf above the chair the hair on my neck stood up. It was a doll, also dressed entirely in black. (There was that feeling again. The doll was watching me with those empty eyes.) There was a silver tray on a round table by the side of the chair. On the tray was a card with writing in black lettering on it. I bent down and read it: "Mourning Room." I swear I then heard a cackle. I looked up just in time to catch the doll lifting its head. I quickly left the room and didn't stop until I was outside in the bright and warm sunshine of the living.

A Helping Hand

*I*t was a beautiful morning when Danny set off for a swim at an old dam near Sheet Harbour on Nova Scotia's South Shore. Instead of meeting up with his buddies as usual, he decided to go by himself, ignoring what everyone said about not swimming alone. Danny wasn't too worried about it. In fact, he wasn't worried about much at all. He was a young, strong lad—and the best swimmer on his team.

The water was cool, but the day was hot, and Danny was feeling refreshed as he swam toward the dam. He was concentrating on his front stroke, going through the exercises in his mind, when suddenly an old woman appeared on a large boulder on the bank. Danny looked at her expectantly. He knew everyone in the village, but he was certain he had never seen this woman before. Something inside told him to keep moving, but he shook it off. What could this harmless old woman possibly do to me? he thought.

As he came abreast of her, Danny noticed she tilted her head to the side and looked at him quizzically. "Where you off to boy?" said the woman. Danny had the urge to tell her it was none of her business but he thought better of it. He didn't answer her, and turned to swim away. "I asked you where you off to?" Danny continued to ignore her and quickened his pace. "Don't be so high and mighty young man. You never know when you may need a helping hand," she called after him. He turned his head to look at her one last time, but she was gone. He figured she was upset at his insolence and just kept going on her way.

A few minutes later he reached the old dam. Anxious to sharpen and hone his diving skills, Danny got to it right away. He kept looking around expecting to see the old woman watching him, but he was thoroughly alone. Still, he couldn't get her out of his mind—she reminded him of someone, but try as he might, he could not place her.

Danny stood poised at the highest point of the dam. The water was dark but inviting so he took in a deep breath and dove in. Unfortunately, what Danny hit that day was more than just the water: his forehead struck something below the surface. Danny couldn't move his arms and legs and he fought against losing consciousness. If he did pass out, he would drown for sure. "Yes that's it, float until the weakness and pain passes," he told himself. But when he tried to level his body he couldn't get his legs up. Twice he went under and twice through sheer force of will he got himself back to the surface. He struggled to make it to safety but his strength was waning. Unless there was help or a miracle, he feared he would not make it.

Suddenly, a hand broke the surface of the water and reached for him. Through hazy eyes, he saw her. It was the old woman. She smiled, "Take my hand, Danny." How did she know my name? was Danny's thought as he passed out. Minutes later, he woke up safe and sound on the shore of the river. There was no sign of the woman who had saved his life.

Some months later, Danny's grandmother was closing down her summer home and he and his parents went down to the shore to help her pack her things. As Danny was passing the dining room table, he noticed several portraits ready to be wrapped and put away in boxes. One picture in particular caught his attention. He was drawn to it because the face in the picture looked familiar. He stood looking down at that stern face that somehow seemed softer than when had seen it on that summer day. Danny called his parents and grandmother into the dining room. "When I told you I was saved from drowning by an old woman, you asked who she was. I didn't know at the time, but I do now." Danny pointed to the picture of the old woman and said "That was the lady I saw that day. She was the one who helped me."

Danny's grandmother stepped closer to the table. She looked down at the picture, shaking her head in disbelief. "There must be some mistake, Danny," she said. "That's my great grandmother, your great,

great, great grandmother. She's been dead for a very long time." Danny looked at the picture then back to his parents and grandmother and said: "Dead, yes, but not gone."

The Bear's Den

The Bear's Den B&B is located on Water Street in Shelburne. The two-hundred-year-old home is presently owned and operated by Elizabeth Atkinson, who told me, with a chuckle, that one of the owners back in the 1950s came to Shelburne to compete with her father in the jewellery business—"Now I own his house. That's poetic justice for you." When I bring up the topic of hauntings in the house, she tells me that there is not one but two old ghosts living there, and that both are male.

"I became aware of the possibility that the old place was haunted when the knocking started and the doorbell began ringing at all hours of the day and night," she said. The first few times the doorbell rang, Liz started to rush to the door, but there was never anyone there. A visiting friend reassured Liz, saying, "It's only kids," but Liz suspected differently: When she looked out, no footprints in the snow led to her front door.

The presence of ghosts in Liz's new home and place of business was brought to her attention one evening while she entertained two guests from Ontario and Quebec. The woman from Quebec sat up suddenly and said, "I have a message for you from the old man seated over in the corner of the room. He wants me to tell you he doesn't like all the commotion and he wants everyone to leave his home." Liz's response, besides surprise of course, was one of indignation. "Well, you can tell the old man I am certainly not leaving. This is my home now."

Soon after, one evening while Liz prepared supper in the kitchen a guest entered and asked Liz about "the peculiar markings on the ceiling." When Liz looked up, she saw three markings, each about three feet long. How they got there remains a mystery, and it took a lot of elbow grease to remove them.

Liz has never actually seen the ghosts, but she knows when they're near. One night while seated before her bedroom mirror, she was tapped on the shoulder. She remembers an odd smell and a brush of cold air, but she could not see any but her own reflection in the mirror.

Liz Atkinson maintains the two ghosts are locals—one is the former owner and rival jeweller who came to town in the 1950s, the other is a neighbour from across the street who apparently came to visit the other ghost and never left. He's the ghost that sits in the window box watching people going by. Not everyone can see him, only those in tune with the spirit world, like the guest who woke up to find someone sitting in a chair watching him. The only thing he remembers about the ghost was the way he was sitting…like Rodin's "Thinker." Perhaps the ghost was thinking of ways to rid the house of humans!

Nervous Nellie

The Fagan family lived on Nova Scotia's Eastern Shore. A loving, close-knit family, they lived a quiet and contented life. There was only one problem. Things were never where they were supposed to be, and often, when someone in the family got up in the morning, they found cups and saucers in shattered pieces on the floor. Furthermore, the family members always had to be careful about where they stepped, as quite often things seemed to be spilled on the floor. Yet none in the family claimed to be responsible for the accidents.

One of the Fagan daughters offered an explanation. "Maybe, we have a ghost in the house." Her younger brother giggled.

"Ridiculous," said the father. "There are no such creatures as ghosts." No sooner had he said this when a cup fell off the sideboard and smashed on the floor. The mother jumped, the daughter smiled and the brother giggled again.

"Now, now, that was a just a coincidence, nothing more."

"Yes father," said the daughter as she left the kitchen on her way to school. "Whatever you say."

The mother had had quite enough of this. The first few accidents she had chalked up to childishness, but she was beginning to put more faith in her daughter's explanation. "What if she's right? What do we do then?" she asked her husband. Mr. Fagan reassured his wife. "Don't worry yourself about it. There are no ghosts in this house."

Putting on a brave face for the family was one thing, but the father was also having second thoughts about all the "coincidences" and "accidents" that kept occurring. One day, he went so far as to check all of the shelves in the house. They were all perfectly level. Yet the odd things continued to happen. It was getting harder to convince himself that a ghost was not at work in the Fagan household. Finally, with the urging of his family and his ultimate hope to prove them wrong, he decided to research the history of their house.

Mr. Fagan went to the provincial archives in Halifax and spoke to a local historian. Together, they managed to piece together the history of the family's house. A sea captain by the name of Eli Philpotts had built the house in 1833 for his bride, Nellie Fortune. Nellie, a little slip of a thing, was skittish around people. The couple rarely entertained because Nellie was so nervous that she often dropped things. Eli was devoted to Nellie and he never complained, even when she broke their best china.

They lived happily together for many years, doting on each other and laughing at Nellie's clumsiness. One day, however, tragedy struck, and Captain Eli's vessel didn't return to port. The vessel, its crew and its captain were never heard from again.

After her husband's ship failed to return on the appointed day, Nellie spent all her waking hours sitting at the window scanning the horizon. It came to pass that Nellie hadn't been seen around town for three or four days. Neighbours found this odd and became concerned. Some of them decided to go to the house and investigate. They found her sitting in her seat at the widow, dead, with her eyes still fixed on the horizon. She spent her last moments on earth waiting and watching for her beloved husband.

When the undertaker and his assistant were bringing Nellie's body downstairs, they swore they saw her ghost standing in the kitchen watching her body being removed. They couldn't leave fast enough when they heard a dish crash to the floor!

Mr. Fagan decided it was best to tell his family what he had discovered: "I have checked out the problem and, as unbelievable as it seems, we do appear to have a ghost to contend with. But, a harmless one. Her name was Nellie Philpotts. Her husband was a sea captain who was tragically lost at sea and Nellie never got over his drowning." Just then a cup dropped to the floor. There was a long silence.

The precocious daughter smiled and said, "Good evening, Mrs. Philpotts, or should I say...Nervous Nellie?"

At the shore

*J*ohn and Annabel needed to get away from the city. They loved Halifax, but the cottage they had rented near Mushamush Lake in Lunenberg County was perfect and they were looking forward to the peace and quiet of a month's holiday at the shore. Everything seemed too good to be true.

It was raining when the strange occurrences began. Only Annabel heard it, the sound of a car's engine—something old, like a model "A"—followed by voices. It wasn't the tinkling laughter of children that Annabel heard; it was the sound of children crying coupled with the desperate voices of adults hollering. Annabel told her husband she thought it was coming from somewhere on the river.

But John was skeptical: he heard nothing and couldn't understand why Annabel was so upset. When she told him what she heard, he thought it might be some kids playing a trick on them. He went to the window to see, but with the heavy downpour and the darkness and trees, it was impossible to see clearly. John returned to the living room, telling Annabel he didn't see anything.

This haunting happened every afternoon at precisely the same time. It was becoming unbearable for Annabel and she began to dread the afternoons. She was becoming very nervous, glancing at the mantle clock obsessively as the hands moved closer and closer to four thirty. Finally, she couldn't take it any longer, and said to her husband, "That's it, John. I can't stay anymore. Listening to the pathetic cries of the children wrings my heart out."

John didn't argue with her. He also had enough and was finding it difficult to relax as they had hoped. Although he still had not heard the voices that Annabel spoke of, he couldn't bear her agitated state. It was decided. They hurriedly packed up their belongings and threw everything into the car. They were almost ready to leave when an old man came up from the shore. "Leaving so soon? Can't say I'm surprised," he said. John looked at the old man for a moment, trying to figure out what he meant. When the old man didn't explain further, John asked: "And just what do you mean by that?" John thought maybe this stranger knew more than he was saying—maybe he was even responsible somehow. "This place is haunted of course," replied the man. "Not the cottage itself, but the river. Which one got the special gift or the curse as some call it? Ah, yes, the little lady. I can see it in her eyes." John was becoming irritated. "Gift? Curse? We're not interested."

But Annabel was very interested. The old man didn't look at John when he spoke again. He looked directly into Annabel's troubled eyes and told this haunting story: "It happened a long, long time ago. Wintertime, it was. This family had a father, mother, and five little ones." Here he paused for a long time, and stared at the river."...and a grandfather whom the children called Poppy Jay. Well, they all climbed into their brand, spankin' new car and headed for town. They decided to take a short-cut across the frozen river. Halfway across, the ice gave way and the car went down like a rock with everyone in it."

Annabel knew his story to be true at once. "Are you telling me that what I hear are the ghosts of those who drowned?" The old man nodded. John turned to place the last of their belongings in the car. With his head halfway in the trunk, John said. "Yes it is a terribly sad story, but nevertheless, we're packed now and are returning to the city."

When Annabel turned to thank the old man, he was gone. "Where did he disappear to?" she wondered. Annabel suddenly stopped. Holding several book in her arms, she looked at the cottage, then the river, and back to John. "You don't suppose do you, John, that he could be...the grandfather?"

The Ghost in the Attic

*T*here are very few old homes that don't have a past, mysterious or otherwise, and it is the past that haunts the house in this story.

Charles and Margaret Wicks, who lived in Toronto, had Maritime roots and decided to abandon big-city life and spend their retirement years in a rural setting. So off to Nova Scotia's coast they went.

The search for a new home began, and soon they discovered wonderful old mansion in the Annapolis Valley. It wasn't for sale, but they could lease it, so they did just that.

It wasn't long after they were settled in that Margaret realized there was something in the attic—living or otherwise. During supper one evening she broached the subject with her husband, Charles.

"I don't know if you are aware of it, Charles, but we have a problem in the attic." "Leaking?" said Charles.

"No. Something is living up there. I heard noises and things being moved about."

"What kind of noises?"

"Well, this morning, for instance, I was having some tea when I heard something being dragged across the floor. Even stranger, I think I heard crying."

"Hmmm," said Charles. "You think someone is living in the attic rent-free? We can't have that now, can we?"

Margaret looked at her husband. *Figures,* she thought. *Charles the former banker always thinking of cost—no one gets a free ride!*

"So," she said, "You'll check it out?"

"Certainly, we'll both check it out right after supper."

Just then they heard a thump.

"See," said Margaret, "what did I tell you?"

Charles got up from the table, stretched, and said, "Let's see what's up there now."

Halfway up the stairs, Charles turned to Margaret and asked, "I don't remember checking the attic before, do you?"

"We didn't. Remember you said, 'we're leasing the place, not buying it, and anyway we're not going to live in the attic.'"

"Ah, yes, I do remember now. Pays to check, though, my daddy always said." Margaret rolled her eyes at that. Charles let out a great sigh and took the last two steps to the attic door.

Charles's fingers fumbled around inside the doorframe until they came in contact with the light switch. The room was large and filled with boxes of all sizes and descriptions. Beds propped up against the walls and mattresses were piled high in a corner. Below the only window in the room Margaret noticed a huge steamer trunk—and something else. "My god in heaven—a child! Oh, my, my," she said "Do you see her, Charles?"

"See what?"

"The child sitting on the trunk by the window."

"No," Charles said, "I see no one. You're seeing things."

"I'm not. I can see her, plain as day. She's wearing a black dress with a white collar and her feet are bare. She can't be more than eleven or twelve, and may even be younger. She must be a ghost!"

"How do you know she's a ghost?"

"Because she's fading in and out. God almighty—we have our very own ghost."

"How come I can't see her, then?"

"Maybe because you're not a believer. Ever think of that?"

The ghost liked Margaret immediately, but Charles she wasn't so sure of. She decided it would be best to disappear altogether until she knew how they really felt about spirits and if they could accept one in the house.

"Ah, she's gone. You must have scared her, Charles."

"Me? How could I scare her if I didn't even see her?"

"Ghosts know," was Margaret's reply.

That night in bed, Margaret's mind was racing. She would get to know the ghost. Find out her name, everything, especially how she became a spirit—and then later, when they got to know each other better, who knew what could happen? Margaret's one sorrow in life was not having children of her own. Feeling hopeful, she finally fell sleep.

The next morning, just as soon as Charles left for town, Margaret immediately went up to the attic. There was no sign of the young ghost girl anywhere. *Maybe I was imagining it*, Margaret thought. *But she seemed so real.* Just then her right hand became very cold. When she looked down she nearly passed out. Beside her was the same girl she had seen the day before. The ghost had Margaret's hand in hers. At first Margaret could see the girl's lips moving, but she could not hear what she was saying. She leaned in closer, in time to hear the ghostly words, "My name is Cassie Fielding."

"I'm very happy to know you Cassie Fielding. My name is Margaret Wicks."

The ghost of Cassie Fielding led Margaret over to the steamer trunk where they sat down. "How old are you, Cassie?"

"I'm eleven going on twelve."

"You have an English accent. So you must be from somewhere in England?"

"I do? I mean, have an accent? Because yes, I'm from London."

"How did you become...ah—how did you become...a..."

"A ghost? My family and I were coming over to spend our holidays in New York, and also Halifax where my father's cousin lives. I can't remember the name of the ship but I remember it was new and large."

The Titanic! Margaret thought.

"The ship was so beautiful," Cassie said, "so much brass, and so many mirrors, and long winding stairways. Because it was so huge, my brother and I would play hide and seek. Father told us to be careful because if we got lost on such a big ship we may never be found again. And he also told us that if something terrible should happen during the crossing, we were to stay together. 'If you get separated, stay put and we'll come for you no matter how long it takes,' he said to me again and again. So I must stay here until father comes for me.

"There must have been an accident of some kind. I remember I couldn't sleep so I snuck up on deck. It was very calm that night.

The sky was clear and full of stars. I was standing by the ship's railing, looking down at the water and I saw all these huge chunks of ice floating by. The ones that were poking up through the water looked like church steeples—I wondered how big they were below the water. Suddenly, there was a big bump. It felt like the ship ran into something. Then it began tilting, and I fell over the railing. I don't remember anything after falling. When I opened my eyes, I was in this room. How I got here, and why, I don't know. It took me a long time to remember what had happened and understand that I had drowned. But now I need to know: where were my parents and my brother? Were they saved?"

Little Cassie Fielding then began to cry. Without thinking, Margaret took the ghost into her arms and rocked her soothingly. She decided then and there that she would adopt Cassie Fielding, ghost or not. Cassie would become the daughter she never had. She knew, of course, that Charles would balk against such an unnatural situation, telling her she was crazy. "Besides," he'd argue, "officially it can't be done." *Well see, we'll see,* she thought to herself.

When Cassie stopped crying, Margaret asked her how long had she had been in the attic.

Wiping her eyes, Cassie said, "A very long time—years. I've tried to leave but I could never get the door open. I could never turn the knob."

"What about stepping through the door? You know, you're a spirit. Have you tried that?"

"No! It never occurred to me. Would that work, do you think?"

"Never know 'till you try. Want to?"

"Yes." But when the ghost girl reached the door, she paused.

Margaret whispered, "Go ahead. What have you got to lose?"

Cassie stepped back, smiled at Margaret and walked straight through the door—and just as quickly, stepped right back in.

"I did it, I did it!"

"Want to go down stairs and look around?"

"Oh yes. But the man that was here yesterday…is he down there?"

"You mean my husband? Charles is a big pussy cat. Anyway he's not in the house and won't be back for another hour or so."

Gingerly Cassie followed Margaret down the long and winding stairs to the front hall. When Cassie reached the front door she pulled the curtains aside and peeked out into the world she no longer belonged to.

"Come," said Margaret, "I'll show you the rest of the house."

When the tour was over, Margaret stood by the stove waiting for the water in the kettle to boil. "We'll have a nice cup of tea…I'm sorry, do ghosts…?"

Cassie smiled. "There is no need for a ghost to eat or drink. You go ahead."

Cassie sat at the kitchen table watching Margaret prepare the tea. Marvelling at her wispy form perched there, Margaret wondered what it was like being a spirit. Cassie said, "I can guess what's on your mind. Are you wondering what it's like, being in my world?"

Margaret nodded. "You never get hungry, or thirsty or tired. Well, that's not quite true. You do get tired of the sameness. The worst part, though, is the loneliness."

Cassie told Margaret that she could not explain why she ended up in that particular house. Perhaps because it was so old, isolated and close to the sea. "Maybe that's why spirits are attracted to such a place. There could be others—and will be—others. I'm sure of that."

"Well," said Margaret, "as of this moment, Cassie Fielding, you are part of the Wicks family." Cassie's ghost smiled and crossed over to where Margaret was standing, hugging her around her waist. Margaret couldn't feel anything—just a sensation of coldness—but she didn't mind.

The sound of a car pulling into the Wickses' driveway startled

Cassie's ghost, who was about to flee back to the attic. "No stay," said Margaret. "Sit over there, invisible if you like, and observe. You'll find Charles to be a nice person after you get to know him."

"I'm back," Charles greeted his wife, hanging his coat on a kitchen chair. "Guess who I ran into in town today? Actually, never mind, you'd never guess his name in a million years. I met Mr. Crabbe. Remember, he's the one who got us interested in this place? He told me there's a good chance the owners will sell. Seems one of the owners passed away and the other doesn't want to come back and live here alone."

"That sounds wonderful!" exclaimed Margaret.

"Well, here's the thing—I'm not sure if it is so wonderful," said Charles.

"Meaning?"

"Something else I found out. Do you know how many people have died in this house?"

"No. How would I?"

"Twelve, that's how many, an even dozen. That's a lot of people dying in one house, don't you think?"

"I suppose so, if the house were relatively new. But this house is over two hundred years old. If twelve people have died here during that span of time, it's fairly normal, don't you think?"

"Perhaps, but that's not the case here. All twelve died during the last ten years, and all were accidental."

"'Accidental'?"

"Tripping, falling, dying mysteriously in their sleep, choking on food and accidental poisoning."

"And just what are you trying to say?"

"Well, doesn't it seem strange to you that all these people died the way they did? That's all I'm saying. By the way, any activity from our non-paying guest up top?"

"She's sitting across from you, listening to everything, and I must say with interest too. I do think you scared her a couple of times though. She's there on the stool."

"What?!" A visible shudder passed through Charles's body. "Margaret, that's not the least bit funny."

"I'm not kidding. We've had a long talk, Cassie and I, and we've agreed that she no longer has to stay in the attic. As a member of this family, she has the run of the house."

"What do you mean, a member of this family?"

"Cassie is now a member of our family. It's kind of an in-house adoption, if you will."

"Come on, there's no one there. Look, the stool is empty. Who are you kidding?"

"Cassie Fielding Wicks, meet your in-house father, Charles Wicks."

Slowly a form began to take shape. Charles's eyes widened and his heart began pounding as the shape of a young girl with green eyes and hair the colour of gold slowly took form. She slid off the stool and came toward Charles. Not knowing what she was going to do, Charles backed away. "Stay away from me!" he shouted. "Margaret, for the love of—I don't believe in such things."

"Well," said Margaret, "seeing is believing. Now act your age. She's not going to put a spell on you or make you disappear. Look at her. She wants to be your friend. Speak to her."

"Speak to her? I wouldn't know what to say!"

"'Hello, Cassie' would be nice."

Charles's greeting was rather more garbled. What he actually came out with was, "Hello there, you girl. Are you really a ghost you are?"

Margaret looked at Cassie and they both looked at Charles and laughed. And then Charles gave a weak laugh. "Okay," he said, "This isn't natural or normal, and I don't even know if it's happening—but we'll see, we'll see."

The next morning Margaret convinced Cassie to accompany her while she shopped. Cassie froze at the thought of leaving the safety of the house. Margaret finally convinced Cassie to go along. But would Cassie agree only if she could remain invisible.

"Absolutely," said Margaret. "How could I explain you to people otherwise?"

Charles gave a faint smile. He told Margaret that while she and Cassie were out, he'd be down in his workshop catching up on some projects. Charles stood in the doorway watching his wife's car disappear over the rise. When he opened the basement door he thought he heard footsteps coming down from upstairs. He stopped and listened. Five seconds passed. Ten. Fifteen. He heard nothing but his own heavy breathing.

And in the car, if Cassie were visible, Margaret would have seen her small body stiffen and her face fill with fear. Cassie whispered: "We must return to the house immediately, Mr. Wicks is in danger. I will leave the car now. Please turn around and hurry."

"Danger? What kind of danger?" Margaret asked quickly.

"I can't explain now. You must go back."

When Charles was about to place his right foot on the basement step, he felt an explosion in his head. He tried desperately to stop from falling but couldn't keep his balance. Then suddenly, it was as if he fell upon a cushion of air—the fall was broken and he was laid gently on the cold concrete floor, where he passed out.

Cassie looked up from the man whose life she had just saved to see a demonic ghost coming straight at her throat. Cassie sidestepped and the creature slammed into the far wall, giving the girl the few precious seconds she needed. She saw Mr. Wicks' electric sander on the workbench and she quickly disconnected it from the power cord, which was plugged in the wall. As the spirit came flying across the room with its claw-like fingers reaching for Cassie, its hot, putrid breath upon her face, she drove the wire into its chest. There was a guttural howling and the evil spirit exploded in a ball of fire. All that was left was a pile of smouldering clothing.

Cassie heard a car door slam, and Margaret ran into the house, calling Charles's name. "Down here! We're in the basement!" Cassie called back. Margaret hurried down, and when she saw her husband's still body on the floor, she became faint, but managed not to pass out.

"He's unconscious," Cassie said. "But he'll be okay."

"What happened? And whose clothes are those burning?"

"Oh Margaret. I'm so sorry I didn't warn you earlier. These clothes belong to an evil spirit who also lives here. She's the one responsible for those twelve deaths that Mr. Wicks spoke about. I was intending to tell you about the evil spirit but I wanted to wait for the right moment. I was almost too late, and I'm so sorry."

Charles was coming around, moaning. Margaret lifted his head onto her lap, and to make sure he wasn't suffering from a concussion, asked him, "How many fingers do you see, and what is my name?" Sarcastically he replied, "Your name is Suzanne, you're holding up six fingers, and I want to know what just happened! I'm at the top of the steps, and suddenly something hard hits the back of my head and down I tumble. But I remember I didn't fall all the way down. Something like a cushion of air broke my fall. It was like I was floating."

Margaret didn't say anything. She looked over at Cassie and smiled. Charles caught the smile and turned toward Cassie. "It was you that stopped my fall, wasn't it?"

"Yes, it was I."

"Well then," said Charles, "I suppose you have an explanation for all this?"

"But first," suggested Margaret, "let's go upstairs and get Charles a little more comfortable."

Once they were all seated around the kitchen table, Margaret and Charles looked at Cassie expectantly.

"I could easily vanish, you know," she said, "and that would be that."

"Yes," Margaret gently replied, "But you're not like that, are you?"

"No. Well, all the years I lived here nothing happened. It was even boring, you know. Then she arrived—the evil spirit, I mean. There was an awful thunderstorm that night. I knew immediately that another spirit had come into the house, because the feeling of the place changed. It became dark and foreboding. I not only kept myself invisible but I hid inside that mirror in the attic, and watched and waited. I didn't have to wait long. The room filled with a heavy odour, like dead flowers. And then I saw her. She was tall and ugly and she wore a long black skirt with a black shawl over her shoulders. Her hair was as black as the scowl on her face and it was parted in the middle and fell to her shoulders. She must have known there was another spirit somewhere in the house, as she searched the room so carefully. I froze when she came to the mirror and stopped. And for a moment I felt she saw something else besides her own image in the mirror. I held my breath, waiting. She leaned forward, searching, but then turned away and left the room. If I could have left that room I would have, but I had to wait for father to come for me.

"Well, one morning not too long after she arrived, I heard voices and people moving around downstairs. I crept to the top of the stairs and observed an elderly couple listening to a man telling them about the charms of this house. They nodded in agreement, shook hands with the man, and a couple of days later they moved in. The first tragedy happened very soon. The old man came out of his bedroom, and the demon spirit came up behind him. When he reached the top of the stairs she pushed him and he went headlong down the stairs. It was awful. The evil spirit stood at the top of the stairs laughing at the old man on the floor, and I heard it all happening! I wish I could have helped then, but I didn't even know I could leave the attic.

"Again and again over the last ten years, I have listened to nice, innocent people dying, without being able to help them. And then you came, and you were so kind, and you taught me how to leave the attic, and oh—I wanted so much for you to stay. I should have warned you, but I couldn't bear to lose the only friends I had in all these years.

Will you forgive me?"

Surprisingly, it was Charles who spoke first. "Forgive you? Cassie, you just saved my life. Now, those other people who died, they weren't your fault. I reckon now you have got rid of that evil spirit for good, and you can relax and—well, like Margaret said, we never had our own children…"

Charles's voice trailed off as he realized Cassie had stopped listening. He followed her gaze across the kitchen to the back door, which had blown open suddenly in a gust of wind. There stood three ghostly figures. Cassie jumped from the table, ran to the newcomers, and embraced the tallest. At this point, all three figures became more solid, and Margaret and Charles realized what was happening.

"Oh Charles, they've come for her! I don't know whether to laugh or cry."

Cassie looked truly happy, and was whispering excitedly with what must have been her brother. Her parents—her real, ghostly parents—were beaming down at their long-lost daughter. Margaret and Charles couldn't help but be happy for their little ghost.

Cassie's father thanked Margaret and Charles for caring for his daughter. Margaret invited them all to stay but her invitation was refused; the family had to return to England as soon as possible.

Cassie hugged Margaret and told her that she would never forget her, and that she would always be her earthly mother. Margaret had tears in her eyes when she thought of what lay ahead. "I'll never see you again, will I?"

"Never is a long time. Perhaps we'll meet somewhere later." When Cassie turned to say goodbye to Charles, he was waiting with open arms for a hug from this girl he had barely believed in a few hours before.

"It is time," called Cassie's father. "We must hurry."

Margaret and Charles walked with Cassie to the veranda, where her parents and brother were waiting. They watched as the Fielding family disappeared inside a swirling bright light that lifted them skyward. They stood there watching, transfixed, until the four lights disappeared in the night sky. The couple turned to go back in. From a distant corner of the house they heard a thumping sound, then silence.

Footsteps

A young couple, David and Helen, stood on the veranda of a beautiful house in Truro discussing the age and history of the house with the real estate agent. "Old, said the agent freely, "very old indeed. Built in 1810 as a matter of fact." The agent told the couple that the same family had stayed in the house for those years. Then, hesitantly, she told them the home had remained vacant for quite a long time because of a tragedy. When they inquired as to what happened, David and Helen were told only that a murder had been committed. The agent was reluctant to go into any more detail, and changed the topic by asking them if they would mind living so far from town and neighbours. "The nearest neighbour is two miles away and the town itself, seven," she said. David said that he and his wife would welcome the privacy. The real estate agent unlocked the front door and showed them inside.

They checked all the rooms. Helen peeked into every nook and cranny. There were no hidden passageways, no dark hallways leading to open trapdoors, no closet walls that fell away, and no unexplained shadows passing on the stairway. It was a simple, plain old house that needed some attention. David noticed only the old house smell, but he was more preoccupied with the financing. He saw the place as a good investment, and decided they would move in immediately.

A few uneventful days passed after the move; then, just after dinner one night, as Helen stepped out into the hall, a sudden rush of cold air pushed hard against her face, and she had the feeling of being unwelcome. Her misgivings about their new home grew. It wasn't so bad when David was home but when he left for work or had to go out of town on business, Helen felt uncomfortable being alone in the house. She felt like she was being watched by someone who was right behind her all the time. Several times she thought she caught a movement out of the corner of her eye, but when she turned her head, there was nothing there.

One day not too long after they had moved in, Helen was alone, making the bed upstairs, when she heard footfalls climbing on the steps. She stopped and listened, her heart beating loudly. She came out of the bedroom cautiously but there was no one on the stairs. She could see nothing, it was true, but she could still hear the sound of fading footsteps! Helen suddenly became weak. She would have fallen head long down the stairs if she hadn't grabbed the railing for support. She sat down quickly, wrapping her arms around her knees, and rocked back and forth, afraid of what might be in the house with her.

When her husband arrived home from work that evening, she told him what had happened. She was convinced the place was haunted. David laughed, telling her that it was probably just the excitement of a new place, and the power of suggestion.

That night in bed, unable to sleep, Helen ran through the day's events in her mind; she wasn't so sure it was just her imagination or the excitement of a new place. She was certain that what she'd heard that morning was real.

Rolling over on her left side to face the wall, she suddenly found herself looking straight into the eyes of a child. It was standing so close to the bed that Helen could feel its cold breath on her face. The child touched Helen's cheek with the tip of her finger, whispering, "Mummy, is that you?" Helen stiffened. The little girl stepped back—right through the wall until she was gone. Helen muffled a pitiful cry with her fist pressed to her lips. She didn't want to awaken her husband—he would only say she'd dreamt it.

Many questions swirled through Helen's mind as she fixed her eyes on the wall where the child had disappeared. This explained the footsteps this afternoon, she thought to herself. She could not stay here! How was she going to convince her husband that the house was haunted and they would have to leave?

First, she decided, she would have to find out who the child was and why she was haunting the place. Something terrible must have happened. That was it: when David left for work in the morning, she would find out all she could about the family that had lived in the house and the murder that had taken place.

The next morning, Helen was in her bedroom getting ready to go into town to the local newspaper office when the room suddenly went ice cold. An inner voice told her to run but it was too late. The mirror she was looking into smashed to smithereens. As she turned to flee, an unseen force attacked her and held her down. Her face felt like it was covered in cobwebs, and no matter how she tried, she couldn't pull them off. She heard footsteps on the stairs and the whining voice of the child calling out, "Mummy, Mummy where are you? Don't leave me." Helen got down on her hands and knees, dragging herself into the hallway and down the stairs. When she reached the bottom of the stairs she managed to get the front door open and she broke free. She collapsed on the ground. She wanted to run as far away from the place as she could but she was too weak to move any farther.

From around the corner of the house a tall man carrying an axe walked slowly toward her. Thank God, Helen thought. Another living human being. She assumed he was a woodsman by the plaid shirt and breeches he wore.

Helen was too weak to get up. The stranger removed the axe from his shoulder and cradled it in his arms, like he was holding an infant. Helen shivered, not from the chill in the air, but from what he might do with the axe, but fear left her body when she looked up into his friendly face. He smiled down at her before he spoke.

"I was wondering as I came around the house why you were sitting on the ground and then I remembered the chilling history of this house." Helen explained her experience with the spirits inside. The stranger suggested they go inside where it was warm, jokingly telling her that even ghosts were afraid of a man carrying an axe.

Helen was reluctant to re-enter the house, but something about the man's demeanor made her feel safe, and she found her courage returning. Once they were seated inside, Helen asked the man to explain what he had meant when he had mentioned the "chilling history of the house." She begged him to tell her the story. He provided her with the grisly details.

"An escaped patient from the insane asylum hid in the woods for weeks and when he thought it was safe to come out, he snuck inside this house while the family slept. He then crept upstairs and killed them all."

"Was he caught?"

"Oh, yes indeed and hanged as well. There are reports his ghost is also seen around the property." Helen shivered and was thankful that so far she had just run into the ghost of the little girl that afternoon.

They were still seated at the kitchen table when they heard a car drive up. Helen looked at the wall clock. It was near noon. She told the woodsman that her husband was home for lunch, but the stranger wasn't listening.

David hurried up the veranda steps and went inside. He saw his young wife slumped over the kitchen table. He thought she might be napping, but sensed something was wrong. From somewhere upstairs he heard a child's voice whispering, "Mummy, mummy." On the wall, he saw the shadow of what looked like someone holding an axe over his head.

Music to Wake the Dead

The house in this story is long gone, destroyed by fire as, I'm told, most haunted houses are. For the setting, we must return to the 1940s, to a house located in east Guysborough County. The young man of the house—we'll call him "Tim"—loved music. His favourite music at that time was the famous drummer Gene Krupa. Now, Tim preferred sleeping in the attic because there he could play the drums and listen to music without disturbing the family. But he didn't consider others who might be disturbed.

One night, Tim was playing a record on a portable phonograph, and following along on his drums. He was dreaming that one day he might be as good as Krupa when suddenly the arm of the phonograph was dragged across the record, seemingly of its own accord. Before young Tim knew what was happening, the record went sailing across the room and was smashed to pieces against the wall. Sometimes, as they say, music that's played too loud might wake up the dead.

The next day, Tim reported the previous night's incident to his parents. Their immediate response was to blame his friends. "Who else was with you?" they queried. "No one!" he exclaimed. "It had to have been a ghost." But the boy's parents merely laughed at him and would not believe his explanation of a ghostly presence.

There is more to the story, however. This wasn't the first time Tim had experienced supernatural occurrences while in the attic. A few months before, he had seen the blurry outline of a person. He had been dozing at the time, and had thought it was a dream. But when he awoke later, he felt an uneasiness and remembered the vision. His parents laughed and discounted his tale, chalking it up to an overactive imagination.

The very next morning when Tim's mother was cleaning her son's room, she felt a cool breeze sweep past her. Just before she fainted, she saw an impression on the bed, as if someone was sitting on it—someone she couldn't see. At that moment, the mother changed her mind about ghosts, and changed her address, too.

The B&B Ghost

*I*n 1784, George Gracie of Boston gathered up his belongings, including a two-storey log cabin, loaded everything aboard a vessel and sailed off to Nova Scotia's southwestern shore. Like so many other Empire Loyalists before him, he began a new life on Dock Street in Shelburne.

This new citizen of Nova Scotia soon became a member of the House of Assembly. As George Gracie prospered, he rebuilt his humble log cabin into a three-storey Georgian-style house. The Gracie home still stands and is known today as Coopers Inn and Restaurant. It's also a B&B, owned and operated by Joan and Allan Redmond. From the stories I've been told, it's haunted by George. George Gracie, that is.

Before the Redmonds bought the Gracie home in 1994, the family living there asked their friend Pat Ferguson, owner of the Moon Shadow B&B, if she would check on the house and pets while they were away for a weekend. It was pitch black when Pat stepped into the hallway of her friends' home. After fiddling around for the hall switch, she finally got the lights on. Everything seemed to be in order. Pat took care of the pets, then went up the dark stairs to check the bedrooms. The last thing on Pat Ferguson's mind was the idea that someone might be lurking in the shadows. There was certainly no reason for her to believe the place was haunted.

She finished her tour of the upstairs, and went back down to the main floor. She entered the parlour, and stiffened suddenly. She heard footsteps coming down the stairs. Someone else was in the house!

Pat quickly walked from the parlour to the living room, which faced the stairs. When she looked up, she could make out the shadowy outline of a figure standing on the stairs. With her heart pounding, Pat went into the kitchen. The footsteps followed her. Pat didn't wait to see who or what it was. She threw open the back door and ran full speed until she got back to the safety of her own home.

Later, when she got control of herself, Pat realized she hadn't secured the home. She called a friend and together they went back to check on it. When they got there, the lights were off and the front door was locked. But by whom?

It wasn't long after Joan and Allan Redmond moved in that they realized they weren't the only ones living in George Gracie's home. The family became aware of the haunting when one of the Redmond children was cleaning a bedroom and noticed the bed she had just finished making had the imprint of a body imprint on it. Assuming the ghost of George Gracie was near, the child said, "That's it George. If you have to sit, then sit on the settee and not on the bed." From that moment on there was never another visitation from the ghost.

Joan Redmond says she has never seen a ghost in her home, but when she's upstairs in the old part of the house, she has the sense she's not alone.

There were times when overnight guests at the B&B wanted to know the name of the woman who was sitting in an upstairs bedroom wearing nineteenth-century clothes. Another guest told the Redmonds that he was coming downstairs behind a woman in a long dress. He said when she moved the dress made a swishing noise. And when they reached the bottom step the woman disappeared before his very eyes! Other guests complained about radios and television being unplugged and lights being turned on and off in their rooms.

When people check in, the Redmonds never mention the possibility of what could be upstairs. But the sensitive ones always know. And when these gifted people check out, they mention to the Redmonds that their inn is haunted. The Redmonds smile and nod in agreement, "Yes that's what we've been told," they say.

Did Pat Ferguson ever go back to the Gracie home?

"Yes, I did once," she says. "While sitting in the parlour talking with my friend we heard something like a trunk being dragged across the floor of the bedroom directly above the parlour. My friend called up to her children to stop what they were doing. My friend's husband, who was in the kitchen at the time, wanted to know who his wife was hollering at."

"'The children,' she replied. 'Who else? They're dragging something across the bedroom floor.'"

"'Can't be the children,'" said her husband, 'they're here with me. We're making peanut butter sandwiches.'"

Perhaps one of the ghosts *is* George Gracie. And why not? The poor unfortunate man died a horrible and untimely death. He was blind and it's believed that he fell overboard and drowned while on his way to the legislature in Halifax. At the time of his death, George Gracie was in his mid-fifties. He wasn't ready to go and perhaps that's why his spirit still remains on this side of a watery grave.

Wall-to-Wall Music

*H*ere's a Maritime Mystery that Douglas and Huberte Bourque of Middle West Pubnico are plagued with. Their home, which was built in the 1820s and was owned at one time by Huberte's grandfather, is haunted by ghostly music emanating from its walls. The Bourques only hear the music when they're in bed. Hurberte says she and her family have tried but are unable to identify even the instruments, and the music is unlike anything they've heard before.

There are other disturbing things going on in the Bourque home. Huberte often feels a strong presence in her bedroom, as though someone else is there, and has heard footsteps going in and out of rooms, as well as doors opening and closing. Huberte says she's even heard someone calling her name. Another family member saw the shadow of a tall male form in the upstairs hall.

Are the Bourques going to pack up and leave? Not likely. Hurberte says they love the old place and neither spook music nor footsteps in the dark are disturbing enough to drive them out of the house—not yet, anyway.

The Haunted Convent

For five months in 1976, Russell McManus of Truro, Nova Scotia, attended a sales representative marketing course in Amherst, Nova Scotia. The course was held—and the students were billeted—at the former Sisters of Charity Convent on Church Street.

This story begins with Russell's arrival at the convent. It was late in the evening, and he was greeted at the door by a tall, thin man whose name was Ralph. A large wooden crucifix dangled from a leather thong around his neck.

"I do not belong to a religious order," Ralph told Russell. "I'm the caretaker, and since you're a day early and the first to arrive, you can have the pick of any room, except mine."

The convent was huge, with many rooms on its three floors. It housed a large kitchen, libraries, chapels and a number of washrooms. When the caretaker took Russell on a tour of the convent, they came to a large room that had at one time been used as an infirmary. When Russell chose that room to stay in, the caretaker became somewhat upset and said that that particular room was reserved for stranded transients. Russell wondered what had made the caretaker so upset.

Once Russell had chosen another room, Ralph gave him his bedding and invited him into the kitchen for a cup of tea before bed. Then the caretaker went downstairs. While Russell was unpacking, he heard the caretaker coming back upstairs, and the caretaker's bedroom door open and close. Russell went across to Ralph's room to inquire if the tea was ready. The bedroom door was open but Ralph was nowhere to be seen. Puzzled, Russell went to the infirmary, thinking the caretaker would perhaps be there, but that room was empty. It was very cold, too, and Ralph noticed an open window. He closed the window and the door and went down to the kitchen, where he found the caretaker preparing a late-night snack. Russell asked about the open window in the infirmary, but the caretaker told him he had not gone back upstairs.

"Well," Russell said, "There must be someone else in the convent, because that window was definitely open."

"No, it's just you and me. There's no one else in the building."

Russell began to think that either Ralph was lying to him or there was something very strange about this convent. His skepticism must have been obvious, as something changed in Ralph's face.

"Sit down," Ralph said, his voice heavy. "I may as well tell you the whole story."

Russell sat, and Ralph continued: "There was a man in the last class here who took the room next to mine. He was likable, a foreign chap, but very early on he started complaining about hearing noises in his room, of the door opening and closing by itself, and of the room always being freezing cold." The rest of the class teased their classmate about his vivid imagination and considered the whole thing hilarious.

"Now, this particular student awoke around 2 a.m. one night about a week into his course, and saw a priest by his bed reading the last rites of the Catholic Church. The student screamed and bolted from the room and refused to ever go back. He was so upset that another student had to go into the room to collect his belongings. The chap moved out of the convent, and only came in for his day classes, always leaving as soon as they were over. The other students thought someone must have played a joke on him by dressing up as a priest and reading the rites."

As if that tale wasn't unsettling enough, Ralph went on to tell Russell about several other incidents that had led people to believe the convent was haunted. During the Christmas break, everyone returned home for the holidays except Ralph, who always stayed behind to look after the building. He was sitting in his room wondering if he should go to midnight mass or wait until morning, when suddenly he heard someone coming in the front door. As he listened, he heard heavy footsteps coming upstairs. The caretaker sat motionless, listening, then saw a shadow pass by his open door and go into the infirmary. The caretaker got up and went into the infirmary to see who was there, but there was no one in the room—and the window was wide open. He closed it, turned off the lights, and went back to his room, where he spent a sleepless night.

So the reason no one was allowed to stay in the infirmary was clear: Ralph believed it was haunted. Russell felt inclined to agree. Ralph explained that he often checked the infirmary's window: "More often than not, even though I keep it closed, I find it wide open."

Another story about the convent was just as eerie: One night a student ran from his room and down the stairs. Those who heard him followed to see what was wrong. After a brief search the student was found in the darkened chapel praying. Not wishing to disturb his prayers, the other students went back to bed. The next morning he told his fellow students what drove him out of his room: he had woke suddenly in the night to see a small girl standing beside his bed looking down at him. The student became known as "the pacer" after he developed the habit of pacing endlessly in a circle and mumbling to himself.

Fortunately for Russell, his room at the convent was free of anything from another dimension. Across the hall, however, Russell's friend Sandy was having a rough go of it. Sandy was a friendly, easy-going young man. However, one night he hollered, "I don't know who you are or what you are but the lord is my shepherd and I am not afraid of you!" Sandy told his classmates that something pulled the clothes off his bed. Following the incident, Sandy bought a bible and every night he would sit and read from it to the other students.

The students complained of hearing someone walking up and down the hall outside their doors for hours at a time. Whenever they went to check, they could find no one. It was too much for many students, so they moved out.

Simon, an English lad, was quite good at performing magic, and he also knew how to operate a ouija board. One night he invited his fellow students to his room, where he spread out a black cloth with mysterious markings on it. He placed weird-looking objects on the cloth, including one that was pyramid-shaped with a hole in its base into which a black cord was inserted. He told the students to pass it around while he performed some mysterious chants. According to Russell, the object seemed to come alive and some force tried to pull it from his hands. Scared, Russell broke from the circle and left.

One student put his hand next to Simon's on the ouija board. Simon then asked who was present from the spirit world. The answer came from a thirteen-year-old girl. She told them how she died: She was given a red necklace that was made of poisonous Mexican beans. She got into the habit of putting the beans in her mouth and chewing on them. Soon she became very ill. The doctors were unable to determine the cause of her illness. She was brought to the convent in the hopes that the good sisters could help. Unable to breathe properly, the girl kept begging the sisters to open the infirmary window. In the end no one could help her and she died in the infirmary—room 13.

Simon told the spirit she was wrong—there was no room numbered 13 in the convent. Number 36 was the number of the infirmary. But the spirit insisted it was 13. Simon left the room and checked the door to the infirmary. Sure enough, he discovered a raised section on the door; when he scraped the paint off it, he discovered a small brass plaque with the number 13 inscribed on it.

Near the end of the course, Simon went back to room 13 and, using the ouija board, attempted to get information from the girl on the name of the ghost with the heavy footsteps. What they got from her instead were death threats. She became agitated and angry and told Russell McManus he was going to die very soon and for all of them to leave the room.

Russell didn't forget the ghost's threat and thinks it may have been responsible for a near accident that could have been fatal for him. Russell was driving to Halifax and had placed his portfolio on the seat next to him. Some thirty miles past Truro he noticed the portfolio was gone. He immediately pulled off to the side of the highway to check, but when he stopped the car, the portfolio was on the seat again. The delay took two to three minutes.

As Russell continued toward Halifax, he came upon a large logging truck that had crossed over to his side of the highway and jackknifed into the ditch. The gruesome accident had apparently only just happened because the police had yet to arrive. Russell McManus continued on to Halifax, with the feeling that if he hadn't stopped to check on his portfolio things may have turned out just as the convent ghost predicted.

The Hounds Are Barking

*T*here was a time when those who lived on a certain farm in Cape Breton were happy and prosperous, so prosperous that the owner, James MacDonald, was the envy of the countryside.

But tragedy befell the MacDonald family. They were found by visiting neighbours, seated around a picnic table under an apple tree—dead. They were looking skyward with an expression of terror on their faces. There were no marks, no cuts, no bruises, and no evidence of any poison in their bodies. Their deaths remained a mystery. After the funeral, the farm was put up for sale.

Because of the gruesome and bizarre circumstances surrounding the family's death, the farm didn't sell right away. Locals wouldn't go near the place, let alone buy it. Rumours had spread through the countryside that a ghost had murdered the poor MacDonalds. In time, though, a newly arrived family was interested in buying the farm. When John Moore heard tell of a ghost, he dismissed the tale as nonsense: "Ghosts? Ridiculous." he said. "We'll buy the place and in time we'll purchase cattle and horses and we too will become prosperous."

And then the troubles started again. One morning Sarah, John's wife, looked out at the fields, and what she saw took her breath away. The land, fertile and lush just the day before, was rotting away. The orchard trees hung limp and fruit lay rotting on the ground. Sarah turned to her husband with tears in her eyes and asked what was happening. John could not explain it.

Later that evening, while John was in the barn getting the stalls ready for the cattle and horses he had purchased, screams brought him running to the house. When he burst through the kitchen door he found his wife and daughter cowering against the wall, and his two dogs lying completely still by the stove.

"What is it?" said the anxious father.

"There," said Sarah. "They're everywhere."

"What is everywhere?"

"Ghosts—can't you see them?"

"I don't see anyone but you and Lucinda!" The thought crossed his mind that his wife was having a nervous breakdown, but when his daughter told him that she too could see the ghosts, he quickly changed his mind.

"Describe for me what they look like and what they're doing."

Lucinda told her father what she saw: "They're all dressed in black and they're wearing old-fashioned clothes. And Papa, I think they're here for someone's wake."

"Why do you say that, Lucinda?"

"There's a minister holding the hands of an old woman who is weeping."

The father then looked at the dogs. "What happened to the hounds?"

"Well, they were lying there by the stove when suddenly they sprang to their feet and began snarling, and then they fell over—and I think they might be dead. They haven't moved. That's when we saw all these ghosts."

John looked around the kitchen for a weapon of some kind to drive the spirits out of his home and away from his loved ones. *But,* he thought, *how does one fight the dead?* He stepped forward, and with a stern look on his face and with authority in his voice, asked, "Who are you people, and what are you doing here?"

He jumped back when shadows suddenly appeared before him. They began taking on human shapes. John had difficulty seeing the ghosts clearly. One of them stepped forward to speak, and John heard him clearly enough: "Leave this place or perish like the others. This is a death house. It is not a place for the living. Leave while you still can." The ghost then retreated.

The Moore family watched as the ghosts moved silently from one to the other, speaking in whispers. Sarah turned to John and whispered in his ear, "We will not sleep in this house tonight or ever again." He nodded in agreement.

Just before the family drove off, Sarah turned to her husband and said, "Burn it to the ground with everything in it." John Moore doused the house with gasoline and set the place on fire. They drove off without looking back, the echoes of the hounds barking resounding in their ears.

Ghost on the Menu

Credit for this little gem goes to students of Yarmouth Consolidated Memorial High School, who told a version of this story in the law 441, class of 93 book *A Matter of Mystery*.

It's long gone now, but once upon a time, just outside of Yarmouth, there was a haunted restaurant called Eunice's. According to employees, back in the seventies, the ghosts were hotter than the griddle. They were all over the place.

It all started one night when the manager was closing up the restaurant. The whole place inexplicably became filled with the foulest odour imaginable. The manager began looking for the source; when she got to the dinning room, the smell became much stronger. She said it smelled like a combination of manure, hay and other farm odours. She searched for the source of the odour but could find nothing. The next day, the smell still lingered. Could it be that the restaurant was built on land where a farm once stood and the restaurant's dining room was located directly on the spot where the barn was?

There were other incidences when the ghosts let their presence be known. If an employee forgot to turn the lights off, they'd hear about it. One night the assistant manager received a phone call from a woman with a cackle in her voice. She told him, "You left the lights on again and I can't sleep." He ignored the call as there were no homes near the restaurant, but the voice on the other end of the line was relentless. She called again and again. He went back to the restaurant and turned off the lights. There were no more calls from the mysterious woman with the cackling voice.

Many of Eunice's employees complained that they could feel a presence as they entered the restaurant. There was one particular spot the employees refused to go to alone because the cries of a baby could be heard inside the wall. These were not polite ghosts either, not the kind to mind their P's & Q's. On many occasions they'd greet employees with "Hi there," or simply flutter on by, a cold breeze washing over them.

The cook was one employee who had more than her fair share of experiences with the restaurant ghosts. One day, she turned around quickly from the stove and walked right through the ghost of a man who was standing behind her. The cook remembers the ghost was merely an outline and she said she wasn't the least bit frightened. She knew something was there, however, as the trays of bread and rolls were hovering above the counter. Another time, when the cook was at the restaurant early getting things ready for the breakfast trade, she suddenly found the room very cold and filled with an odd smell. The cook moved cautiously toward the lounge area where she saw many men and women dressed in old-fashioned clothes, dancing.

We know that animals are most perceptive when it comes to the spirit world. It would seem children are too. One day a couple came into the restaurant with their young son. While the parents were looking at the menu, the boy, who had been all smiles outside the restaurant, suddenly became very frightened. He cried and screamed that they couldn't stay there because he was scared of something. Maybe the ghosts were unwilling to leave because of the legendary cooking at Eunice's.

Cold to the Touch

"*F*inally, home at last," Nettie Cudmore whispered to herself as she dragged her aching bones up the driveway to the front door. She was still weak from the accident, but with rest and time, she'd be her old self again. What bothered her more than the stiffness and pain in her right hip was how she and her family were treated while in the hospital. She was a forgiving soul but their thoughtlessness was unforgivable. Lying there on those cold tables with only sheets covering her, her husband and three children. And to make matters worse, left alone in that cold room all that time!

The familiar surroundings brought a smile to Nettie's face as she stepped inside the house. Everything was as it should be. A little dusting was all that was needed. The home was passed down to her from her grandparents and those who visited it for the first time marvelled at how beautiful and large the rooms were.

As she made her way to the kitchen, the familiar surroundings helped her bear the pain she was feeling and she was looking forward to some peace and quiet and a good cup of tea. Seated at the kitchen table, Nettie was trying to keep her mind on what her husband told her. But try as she might, she just couldn't remember. And where were he and the children? Did he say something about getting an estimate of what it was going to cost to repair the damage to the car? Yes of course. They're at the garage! Every time she thought of that horrible accident, she whispered a silent prayer. To Nettie it was nothing short of a miracle that no one was killed. Sighing deeply, as fatigue overcame her, she got up slowly and limped into the living room, where she fell onto the sofa. Before she knew it, she was fast asleep.

She wasn't asleep very long when she was awakened suddenly by the sound of heavy breathing. She nearly fainted dead away when she opened her eyes. Sitting on the other end of the sofa staring at her were the cold, expressionless eyes of a panther, as black as night. This can't be real, she thought. I'm having a nightmare. Fully awake now, she tried not to move or breathe. She heard the sounds of hurried footsteps and voices coming down the stairs. The French doors were suddenly opened and the living room filled with the oddest mixture of people she had ever seen. There were midgets somersaulting across the floor while others were climbing on one and another's shoulders. There were musicians over by the piano tuning their instruments and an enormously fat woman with pink hair of all things was repeatedly hitting a "C" note on the piano while exercising her voice. Over by the fireplace a little old man was teaching a half dozen miniature poodles how to jump through a hoop, backwards. A cold chill went through Nettie's body when she realized that everything in the room—from the furniture to the pictures on the wall—was different. *How could that be?* Nettie wondered. And none of them paid the slightest attention to her. Only the panther seemed transfixed by her presence. She needed to find out who these people were and what were they doing in her home.

She got up slowly so as not to disturb the panther. In a stern voice Nettie spoke, "Excuse me. Who are you people and what are you doing in my home?" She looked around waiting for an answer or some kind of response, but no one paid her the slightest mind. It was as if she wasn't there.

Nettie walked slowly in the direction of a young woman who was seated on the arm of a chair talking to a handsome Clark Gable lookalike. When she was close enough to touch the young woman, she stopped. Nettie slowly reached out with her index finger and touched the young woman's bare arm. It was warm! The young woman jumped and jerked her arm away. When she turned her head she had a startled look on her face. Nettie felt she was looking directly through her. The young woman kept rubbing her arm where Nettie had touched her. She then said something to the young man and left the room. Nettie now knew these people were not ghosts because the girl's arm was warm. Everyone knows ghosts are cold to the touch.

Something urged her to look toward the bay window. Her husband and her children were peering in. Nettie wondered why they weren't coming inside. She crossed over to the window and beckoned them to come in but they didn't move. The children, Nettie noticed, were crying. Nettie knocked on the window again, this time harder, and indicated she wanted them inside at once. But still they remained where they were. Her husband held up a newspaper and pressed it against the window. Nettie stared at the headline in disbelief: "*Railway crossing accident takes the lives of entire Cudmore family.*" Nettie Cudmore realized finally that it was she who was the intruder!

Chapter Three

The Missing

Ghosts of the Halifax Explosion

*T*he morning of December 6, 1917, dawns clear and cold. The streets are bare. A God-awful blizzard is still a day away, and the people of Halifax are blissfully unaware that two horrific and tragic events are just moments away from happening. Nature causes one, man the other.

At close to 9:00 a.m., mothers are getting their children ready for school—winter classes in the city begin at 9:30 sharp. Many children suffer from whooping cough, and will stay home, but they will not be protected from the catastrophe that is now just minutes away. Halifax Harbour and the Bedford Basin are filled with ships of war. A ticking time bomb, the munitions ship *Mont Blanc,* is low in the water and moving north through the narrows of the harbour to the basin, where it will join a convoy headed for Europe. Unbeknownst to its crew, the Belgian relief ship *Imo* is moving out of the basin and bearing down on the incoming *Mont Blanc.*

It's now a few minutes past nine. Fathers are on the streets heading for work. Children are also on the streets on their way to school.

In a twist of fate and as a result of a chain of miscommunications, the two ships collide and the face of Halifax is changed forever. As if by design, the bow of the *Imo* slices halfway through the deck of *Mont Blanc,* setting it on fire. The two ships reverse engines to pull apart. The ensuing sparks ignite *Mont Blanc's* precious cargo. The crippled *Imo* drifts toward the Dartmouth side of the harbour. *Mont Blanc,* now on fire and billowing smoke, drifts closer to the Halifax shore. Very few people know of the dangerous goods below its deck.

The time is now 9:05 a.m. The *Mont Blanc* explodes and the blast levels the north end of Halifax. Houses are blown apart or crumbled on their foundations. Two thousand people die. Of this number, five hundred are children.

Some of those were children on their way to Richmond School that fateful morning. After the explosion, one wall of the school was all that remained. Although the school was rebuilt in 1919, it was eventually closed until the mid eighties when Halifax's family court was moved to the building. I spent some time in the building and even though it was crowded with families and lawyers I had a strong sense, an impression if you will, of another presence. John Campbell, the court administrator, felt the same, and he told me about the ghost children of Richmond school:

"We hear the children practicing Christmas carols. We also hear their laughter, their chatter. Other times we hear running footsteps and the slamming of heavy oak doors. Some staff members report seeing children coming down or sitting on the stairs and these workers stand and watch the children until they vanish."

I was seated across from John Campbell listening to this amazing footnote to the Halifax Explosion when I observed the beginning of a smile on his face; he began to tell me of a painter who had a run-in with the ghost children.

It was agreed that the painting would be done at night, when the court building was closed. When John Campbell arrived at his office the following morning, he noticed that not much painting had been done. He understood why when the painter burst into his office.

"That's it," said the painter. "I quit. I won't be back." John Campbell had a pretty good idea why the painter quit, but he wanted to hear him say it anyway.

"While I was painting, objects were moving about the room and when I got down to move the ladder, it moved on its own. That's when I left in a hurry."

The painter was a man of his word. He never returned.

The Amiro Mystery

*T*his story takes place in July 1900. Rosalie Amiro of Pubnico, Nova Scotia, left her home to go into the woods to collect tree bark and woodchips. She was never seen again.

One hundred and three years later, the question is still being asked. What ever happened to Rosalie Amiro?

This much we do know: She left home with a large basket to collect the tree bark and wood chips from trees her husband and other woodsmen were chopping down. She probably ventured close to where her husband was cutting, but, as I understand it, she didn't speak to him, and moved deeper into the woods, away from the woodsman.

She crossed paths with two young girls who were picking blueberries. Wanting company and someone to talk to, Mrs. Amiro invited them along, but they declined as it was close to suppertime and they had to get home. She bade them farewell and took her leave of the girls.

As mealtime drew close, Mr. Amiro, after a hard day's work in the woods, headed home to have his supper. Night came, and still there was no sign of Rosalie Amiro. So out of character was Rosalie's behaviour that a search party was quickly organized—even a wedding party joined in the search for the missing woman, as did the crews of two American fishing vessels that were in port. The search lasted for days and covered miles of the woods. In the end, though, Rosalie Amiro was never found.

What fate befell her?

According to Edward D'Entremont of lower east Pubnico, who included in his "Whisperings of the Past" booklet a description of the area where Mrs. Amiro was travelling, she probably fell into one of the bottomless sinkholes scattered throughout the swampy area. It's pure speculation, but that is all we can do when faced with another Maritime Mystery.

Captain Swaine's Secret

$\mathcal{A}$ deline Colby said goodbye to Toronto, got in her car, and headed for Nova Scotia's south shore and a new life. She had already bought a two-hundred-year-old cottage that had been vacant for many years but was, according to the real estate agent, in surprisingly good condition, considering.

The cottage reportedly sat high above a wind-swept cliff overlooking the waters of the Atlantic. During the several phone conversations Adeline had with the real estate agent, he told her that she was buying a "getaway place," a place of isolation. It sounded perfect to Adeline, and she bought it, sight unseen, and made arrangements with the local bank to hire a handyman to get the place ready for her arrival.

Adeline was forty years old and strikingly beautiful. She was tall and slender, and had what some would call cheekbones to die for. She had sparkling green eyes and warm auburn hair. A graduate of the University of Toronto, she won a job in public relations, moved on to Queen's Park, and kept moving up until she became the woman who was always a step behind the premier of Ontario. People said she had it all, but she was never satisfied or happy—something in her life was missing. She knew what it was, but would never face up to it because of the drastic upheaval it would bring to her lifestyle. But when she saw her on-again, off-again boyfriend arm in arm with his ex in the lobby of the Royal York, she realized it was time for a change.

Adeline decided that day to pack up her dreams and head east to her father's childhood home. She remembered her own wonderful days as a child visiting Nova Scotia, warm summer days at her granny's cottage along the Fundy shore. She never knew her paternal grandfather, who had been lost at sea. When she'd ask her father where he came from, where he was born, he'd lift her high above his handsome head and shout, "Why, child, don't you know? I'm a

Shubieman!" When he was dying he asked to be cremated—and his ashes? He told the family to do what they wanted with them. "Chuck 'em along Highway 401 for all I care." His ashes were safely packed away, and now Adeline and her father's ashes were taking the trip to Shubieland.

Adeline's thoughts and memories of her parents and grandmother brought tears to her eyes. They were all dead now, and for the first time it hit her how truly alone she really was. All that was left of her family were warm memories.

When Adeline crossed into Nova Scotia from New Brunswick, she lowered the car's window and whispered into the wind, "I'm coming home, Granny." Ever since she was a child, Adeline had dreamed of one day becoming a writer. Today would be the beginning of that dream.

Adeline arrived in Indian Harbour in late afternoon. Her plans were to stay with a friend overnight and go on to her new home in the morning. Her friend, Sandy Armitage, was an internationally recognized painter. She was in the doorway waving when Adeline drove up. They first met as children during a summer vacation up on the Fundy shore and remained friends ever since.

Sandy was the one who found the cottage for Adeline. She was also as an interior decorator, so naturally it was agreed that she should decorate the cottage, purchasing only the necessities until Adeline arrived, when they could both go on a shopping spree.

After dinner, Adeline and Sandy put on sweaters and walked the short distance from Sandy's home to the shore, where they sat on huge boulders much like the ones at Peggy's Cove. They talked about everything—except for why Adeline decided to pack it in and come east. High above, several squawking gulls circled over two Cape Islanders coming into harbour. Adeline said, "This place, I mean, I don't know. Somehow it doesn't seem real." Sandy smiled. "You too, eh? It's said the place is haunted by a woman known as the lady in blue."

"Have you seen her?"

"No, but people I know have."

"Do you think· we'll see her?"

"I doubt it."

And then out of the blue Adeline started talking about why she had left Toronto.

"The reason I came east was to get out of a bad relationship, and I also felt a lack of fulfilment in my work. I've always had the urge to write. I've had this dream since I was ten. I don't know if it was a wise decision. I don't even know if I can write, but I have to find out."

"I always said you were meant to be a writer. I could see it in the letters you wrote to me when we were still kids. You made the right decision Adeline, I can feel it."

There was a chill in the air and fog was rolling in over the rocky beach. "Time to go back," Sandy said.

Adeline was up bright and early the next morning, but not before Sandy, who was working on a new canvas.

"We'll have bacon and eggs before you set off."

"Great. And the coffee smells delicious."

Over the breakfast table, Adeline knew by the way her friend was looking at her that there was something on her mind and that she was having a difficult time finding a way of getting it out.

"I know you too well, Sandy, you have something on your mind. Out with it."

"Well, it's just that. Now, it's just a rumour mind you, and yet if something untoward should happened I'd never forgiven myself for not warning—no, not warning—telling you."

"Telling me what?"

"Well there are stories, rumours, that the cottage you bought is haunted. That's why it's been vacant for so long."

Adeline laughed. "Haunted? Ghosts? Sandy, really."

"It's what I've heard, so I thought it was only right that you should know."

"And I thank you on behalf of myself and all those shadowy things that go bump in the night. Really, Sandy, I'm surprised."

"It's okay then? You're all right with it?"

"Of course. I don't believe in all that hocus-pocus anyway."

Sandy stood in the yard waving as her friend drove down the highway. She stayed there until the car disappeared. She couldn't put a finger on it, but she had an uneasy feeling as she went back into the house.

Two and a half hours later, Adeline turned the car onto the long and winding driveway that led to her new home. She noticed a green truck parked by the side of the house. When she got out of the car, a man came out of the house smiling.

"I'm Eddie Colter. The bank hired me to get things in shape for you."

"Yes, Mr. Colter, nice to meet you. I'm Adeline Colby. How's everything? I mean with the house."

"Oh, great. No problem. Everything is ship shape, like my daddy used to say."

Adeline took in the sweep of the ocean. It was so enormous it took her breath away.

Eddie Colter was watching and sensed her nervousness.

"You gotta be real careful when near the cliff's edge ma'am. It's a mighty long drop to the rocks below. Sometimes if you're standing too close to the edge, the wind will sneak up and lift you clear off your feet and down you go. That's why there's them poles staked out along the edge. Something to hold on to if you have a mind to peek over the side."

"What's down there?"

"Two hundred feet of God's air and jagged rocks to fall on. If that don't kill ya, the fierce surf will. And something to remember ma'am, only a fool walks out here when the fog rolls in."

"Well thank you, I'll remember. It will be some time before I find the nerve to get that close. Well then, I'd like to see the inside of the house before I get things out of the car."

"Right, and then I'll help you with your things?"

"The heavy things, anyway."

Adeline was certain she'd feel differently about the place tomorrow, but today she felt somewhat disappointed. She had assumed the cottage would be warm and welcoming. She had thought wrong.

It wasn't that there was anything specific she disliked. From the outside the cottage looked small, but inside it was quite spacious. There were two large bedrooms, the master bedroom with an ensuite bathroom. There was an enormous living room off the dining room and a good old-fashioned kitchen with ample cupboard space. On the west side of the living room there was an alcove facing the ocean, the perfect spot to write her book. Still, she couldn't shake the disappointment she felt about the house's atmosphere. *Oh well, we'll grow to like each other, I'm sure*, she thought.

Before leaving, Eddie Colter offered to continue the handy work, and she accepted readily.

"I left my phone number on the kitchen table, ma'am, just in case." Eddie Colter then saw the slightly alarmed expression on Adeline's face and quickly added, "It pays to be enterprising these days ma'am; early worm and all that."

"Yes. Thank you. I'll have to see what needs to be done first."

"I left a list of things that should be taken care of with the number ma'am. Well good day to ya."

"Good day." There was something about Eddie Colter that bothered her. Something strange. But if the bank people recommended him, he must be okay.

Adeline was surprised when she checked the refrigerator and shelves. Sandy had bought enough cans of food to last the winter— and, Adeline noticed with relief, a sufficient supply of wine, too. After supper, she watched the news, read a while, and fell asleep.

When she woke in the morning, the dream she'd had cluttered her mind. It was a most peculiar one. It had something to do with people arguing over where to hide a body. She also remembered how angry some of the voices had been.

After a shower she went downstairs to the smell of freshly brewed coffee in the automatic coffee pot. "Ain't progress grand," she thought, as she made her way to the living room. She stood looking out the window at the dawn, sipping coffee and looking at the vastness of the ocean, when she heard someone behind her whispering. Adeline's back stiffened. The hand holding the cup began to shake.

My god, she thought, *if I turn—and I must—what will I see?*

Again the whispering. Her heart was racing and she was having difficulty breathing. She finally whirled around to face whatever it was, but there was no one there. *How could that be?* Adeline wondered. *I distinctly heard someone whispering. Maybe somebody got inside and was trying to scare me.* The thought angered her, which in turn gave her the courage to call out, "Hello? Hellooo?" No one. She crossed the living room toward the kitchen and was stopped in the doorway by what she saw. Faint at first, the shapes were beginning to appear. They were of eight men seated at a long table, whispering to each other. And it looked like the men had just come in from the rain. Water was dripping from their knee-high black boots onto the floor. Fear filled Adeline's heart when one of the men turned and looked in her direction. She took a step back. Was he looking at her or someone else? *I must be losing my mind. Am I seeing what I think I'm seeing?* she thought. *Is this something out of the past? Ghosts! Oh god, Sandy's right! The place is haunted.*

Then too, she remembered the dream she had. Now she wasn't so sure it was a dream at all. Maybe it was these same men arguing during the night while she slept. She stood with her back to the wall, just inches from the open door, and listened while her heart pounded. They were deciding what to do with the body of someone who had stolen something from them.

"Throw 'im over the cliff," someone shouted.

"A burial's too good for the likes of 'im. Thievin' from his own."

"Take 'im out when we sail on the morning tide and dump 'im over the side, I says."

"You're the boss, Cap'n Swaine. What do you say?"

"I say we buries 'im in the secret place in the cellar and we bury the gold under 'im. No one will ever find 'im or the gold. And for good measure, I'll put a curse on them that tries to steal what's not theirs." There was hearty agreement to this plan from the other men.

Adeline looked down, fascinated, as a piece of seaweed floated by in a fine stream of water. She stiffened when she heard chairs being pushed away from the table.

"So, it's the cellar for 'em that try to cheat their mates, right?"

"Aye Cap'n, aye!"

Then there was only silence. *Have they gone?* She wondered. *Should I look? What if they're there waiting for me to show my face? What will I do then? Should I intervene? Can I intervene? If I do, will they attack me or will they vanish at the sight of someone living?*

Adeline waited and waited but there was nothing but absolute silence. Three, four minutes went by. *I just have to find out,* she thought to herself. She took in a deep breath and stepped boldly into the kitchen. It was empty. The only evidence that anyone had been there was the eight puddles of water on the floor. Adeline turned and went out the front door, and for the longest time stood staring into the dawn. *Now,* she thought, *now what do I do?*

What she did was go back into the cottage to get her purse and car keys. She then drove down to the village and sat in a coffee shop until the library opened. She also called Sandy. "You were right, the place is haunted," she said, as soon as Sandy picked up.

"Adeline?"

"Yes, it's me. There were eight of them all seated around my kitchen table discussing ways to get rid of a body and bury gold."

"It was only a rumour. I really never believed the place was really haunted. Are you sure?"

"Of course, I'm sure."

"Where are you now? You're not still in the cottage, I hope?"

"No. I'm calling you from a restaurant in the village. I'm waiting for the library to open so I can see if there's anything there about the place."

"I think you should leave and come stay with me."

"Leave? Don't be ridiculous. If anybody leaves, it will be those creepy ghosts."

"Do you want me to come over and stay with you? Please don't ask me to, please."

"Don't worry, I won't. Listen, I have to go. I'll let you know how things turn out. Bye."

A frail-looking young girl seated at the information desk smiled as Adeline approached. "Yes, how may I assist you?"

"My name is Adeline Colby. I bought the Swaine cottage and I'm wondering if you have a history of the place? Something out of the ordinary?"

"Yes, to both questions. Let me see…Ah, here it is. *Places*, written back in the fifties. The Swaine cottage is included because it's one of the oldest homes still standing and because its owner was a privateer. Would you like to see the book?"

"Yes, of course."

Places was a small book, only eighty pages. Adeline found what she was searching for on page thirty-three:

Not much is known of the owner of the cottage, Captain Samuel Swaine, but we do know he was a privateer. In 1790, Captain Swaine built a cottage on the highest point of land in the port town. He said he selected that piece of land so he could keep an eye on those down below, but others believed the reason was so he could haul his booty up over the cliffs without being detected.

Captain Swaine and his crew were lost in a storm off Sable. Not long after his death there were reports that the cottage was haunted. A family of three fled into the night when they were awakened by screams and angry voices coming from the cellar. Rumour had it that there were bodies buried there and that captain Swaine hid his gold under the bodies.

There were a lot of folks who were itching to find out if there was any gold in the cellar, bodies or no bodies, but the possibility of being confronted by the ghosts of Captain Swaine and his men kept them away.

Closing the book, Adeline smiled, thinking, *I don't know about the gold but I sure know about the ghosts.*

In the weeks that followed, there were no further visits from the ghost of Captain Samuel Swaine or any of his maties, as he so affectionately called them. Eddie Colter, however, was around all the time, fixing little things and painting. He showed up at Adeline's door early one morning with a pressing need to repair part of the foundation. The damage was on the inside, and he wanted to get started before the first frost.

"Well, if it needs to be done, of course. How long will it take?"

"Oh, I'd say no more than a couple of days at the most."

"Very well then. When do you want to start?"

"Sooner the better, ma'am. Got everything in the truck."

"Fine. Actually, I'm going out of town tomorrow morning for three or four days and I was going to call and ask you to keep an eye on the place while I was gone. Now you can do both."

Eddie Colter agreed not only to look after the cottage but also to get the place ready for winter, especially the cracks in the foundation.

"And you'll be leaving when, ma'am?"

"Tomorrow morning. I'll fly out of Halifax to Toronto. If everything goes as planned, I should be back by Saturday at the latest."

The next morning, as Adeline drove out of her driveway, she looked for Eddie Colter's pickup, but it was nowhere to be seen. *Slept in, I suppose,* she thought. *Mr. Eddie Colter, there's something about you that bothers me. You have something on your mind other than just handyman's work. But what?*

If Adeline had looked in the window of the wayside restaurant as she drove by, she would have seen Eddie looking out. Eddie watched Adeline's sleek-looking convertible drive out of sight before he left the restaurant. Parking his pickup by the back door of Adeline's cottage, he quickly grabbed a pick and shovel and hurried inside.

By mid-morning Eddie had dug up most of the dirt cellar floor and was beginning to think that both the buried gold and the body were nothing more than a rumour. He was an impatient man and didn't take disappointments lightly. Cursing, he threw the pick against the far wall. He was about to do the same with the shovel when he heard a creaking noise. His mouth fell open at what he saw. The pick had tripped something that unlocked a secret door in the foundation. Eddie moved cautiously toward his new discovery. He got down on his knees and slowly opened the door all the way. He could see nothing but blackness. He hurried back to his truck to get his flashlight. The light fell on a narrow passageway that sloped downward for some three hundred feet.

"Well I'll be a monkey's uncle if it doesn't go all the way to the ocean!" breathed Eddie, as he noticed the water coming up the passageway thirty or forty feet and then retreating. *What a tidal wave couldn't do to this place!* he thought. He laughed out loud when he thought of how devious ol' Captain Swaine was. Got his booty into the cottage without being seen or caught.

Eddie had to bend down as he pushed his way into the narrow passageway. Halfway down, Eddie stopped. On his right was a torn sheet of tarpaulin that covered what looked like an entrance to a room. Eddie ripped off the tarpaulin and sent the beam of light forward. His eyes bulged in their sockets at what he saw. The room was like a mini-warehouse. Against one wall were boxes upon boxes and Eddie, with glee and greed in his eyes, could only imagine what those boxes contained. But his primary interest was where the good Captain Swaine had buried his gold. Eddie was no one's fool. He knew what to look for. Find a mound of earth or even a tiny depression in the earth's floor, and you'll find something buried.

He shone his flashlight across the dirt floor. Aha! There it was, a visible depression. Quickly he crossed the room, fell to his knees, and gently pressed the palms of his hands onto the surface.

"Could this be it?" he muttered. "Could Captain Swaine's gold be buried here?" Eddie went back to the cellar, got his shovel, and returned to the room to start digging. After a few minutes, his shovel struck something solid. He moved the beam of light, and then jumped back. A skull!

Adeline was sitting in the Halifax airport, sipping coffee and listening to the news, when her cell phone rang. The call was from her agent in Toronto, telling her the meeting with her publisher had been postponed until next week.

"So there is really nothing we can do but wait. I hope you understand," apologized her agent.

"Yes, of course. Another hour and I'd have been on the plane, but I can get home today."

Adeline said goodbye to Miriam, went to her car, and wondered if she should go straight home or spend some time in Halifax. She decided to do some shopping in the city and then head home.

It was dark when she pulled into her driveway. There were lights on in the kitchen and cellar. When she got out of the car she noticed the back end of Eddie Colter's truck sticking out from behind the cottage. It looked like he was trying to hide it. There wasn't a sound when she stepped into the front hall. When she got to the kitchen she noticed, annoyed, that Eddie had made himself a sandwich but hadn't bothered tidying up. The door to the cellar was slightly ajar. Adeline listened, but heard nothing. Slowly, she went down the narrow steps into the semi-lit cold and damp cellar. Every inch of the cellar floor was dug up, and there was an opening in the foundation. This did not look like an ordinary repair job. When she got closer and looked inside the narrow passageway, she saw a thin beam of light coming from what she assumed was a room. *Maybe*, she thought, *something happened to Eddie*. She moved slowly down the passageway toward the light. She stopped a few feet away from the gaping doorway and listened. The only sound she heard was the lapping of water against rocks. She looked further down the passageway, but there was only darkness beyond the room. *The passageway must end at the edge of the cliff*, she thought, as she walked into the dimly lit room. She was only a few feet inside when she was struck on the head. She fell toward an opening in the dirt floor, and landed face to face with a human skull.

When Adeline came to, her wrists and ankles were tied. When she tried to free herself she heard someone laughing. She twisted to look behind her and saw her handyman chuckling away.

"You'll never get free, ma'am. When old Eddie ties someone up, they stay tied. I didn't bother taping your mouth, cause who's to hear you down here? Now, here's the thing. If you had stayed away like you promised, I'd have all this here gold stashed away and I'd be long gone. But of course I can't have you telling everyone what I've found, so I've decided that our friend there has been alone for much too long a time and I'm sure he'd love some company, especially one as lovely as you." He gestured to the skull.

Adeline had never begged anyone for anything before, but she was about to when something she saw in the passageway stopped her. Shadows! Eight of them. Eddie Colter saw the expression of surprise and fear on Adeline's face and turned, but it was too late. The ghosts of Captain Swaine and his maties pounced on Eddie Colter. Adeline listened to Eddie's horrible screams as he was dragged down the dark, narrow passageway.

Adeline waited five, ten, fifteen minutes, but heard nothing. She looked around for something to cut the ropes around her ankles and wrists. Her eyes fell upon Eddie's knife. She was about to crawl over to get it when Captain Swaine appeared in the doorway. The sight of him sent a wave of fear through her body. She could hardly breathe and was afraid she was about to faint.

Captain Swaine stood with both hands on his hips.

"Well then, me fair lady, what am I supposed to do with you? It's obvious you were not in cahoots with what we dragged out of here."

How Adeline found the breath to speak then, she never knew. "Eddie Colter? What happened to him?"

"Oh, him? Not to worry ma'am. Eddie Colter has shipped out. He's on the final voyage of life. But you, fair one, as caretaker of my humble abode—"

And suddenly, Adeline couldn't control herself, no matter the consequences.

"Excuse me! But this is legally my home now."

"Of course, of course," said the grinning ghost.

Adeline knew he was patronizing her, but she let it go, not wanting to push too hard.

She watched the ghost of Captain Swaine pace back and forth across the room. She observed him closely, wondering what was on his mind and if he held her future—her life—in his ghostly hands. Then the ghost picked up Eddie Colter's knife and knelt before Adeline. Adeline looked fearfully at the knife, but when she looked up into the eyes of Captain Swaine, she knew he wasn't going to hurt her. He quickly cut the ropes that bound her wrists and ankles.

"I've decided that since—what's his name? Colter. Yes, since Colter was going to murder you, you were not in league with him. Therefore, since you've taken over the cottage, I'm appointing you the keeper of my treasure. It's not that I don't trust you, but to be on the safe side, I shall keep an eye on things. Drop in from time to time, so to speak."

Adeline shook her head violently. "I don't want to have anything to do with it. Take it and bury it somewhere else."

"No, I can't do that. It's here and here it will stay."

He then removed his cap, bowed low and whispered, "Until the next time, adieu, adieu." And with that, he vanished.

Adeline got up and slowly, still dizzy from the knock on her head, made her way back upstairs. When she closed the cellar door behind her, she turned the skeleton key in the lock out of habit. But she knew better, really. She'd just have to live with those intruders from the ghost world, or leave. But she wasn't going to leave anytime soon. *No,* she thought, looking around her, *I'm not leaving yet. This place is just starting to feel like home.*

vanished

*T*his ghost story first appeared in the *Oxford Journal* in 1954 and was brought to my attention by Nancy Huston of Dartmouth, Nova Scotia.

The tale takes place in Westchester Mountain, Cumberland County, Nova Scotia, in the year 1880. The old post road from Truro to Amherst passes over a mountain—and there was a time when people who lived in the area avoided that road as much as they could, because everyone knew it was haunted.

Our ghost has a name: Bill Eagles. He disappeared up on that mountain, but the story does not end there. Naturally Bill's neighbours were concerned when he went missing, so they organized a search party, but couldn't find hide nor hair of Bill. He just vanished—at least, his body had.

It wasn't long after Bill's disappearance that people crossing over the mountain reported seeing a ghost. But no one stayed long enough to find out what it wanted. On one such encounter, Hugh Scott left his sister's home in Truro by way of the post road and headed home to Amherst on horseback. Bad choice. When Hugh reached the top of the mountain he slowed the horse to a walk so he could cut up some tobacco for his pipe. When he looked up, he saw the ghost of Bill Eagles walking beside the horse. Scared nearly out of his wits, Hugh dug his heels into the horse's rump and was off the mountain in no time at all. When he later told his brother William that he had met the ghost of Bill Eagles, his brother asked whether he had talked to Bill to find out why his ghost was haunting the mountain.

"No," admitted Hugh. "I got off the mountain as fast as the horse could run."

"Well," said William, "If I ever meet him, I'll stay long enough to find out what he wants."

A few months later William Scott got his wish. He was travelling along the old post road, near the spot where Hugh had met the ghost. And suddenly, the ghost of Bill Eagles was walking along beside the horse. William Scott, a man of his word, didn't gallop off like his brother and others had. Brave William spoke to the ghost.

"Hello Bill, what is it you want?"

Bill's ghost, apparently relieved that someone had the courage to ask, replied, "I want to be buried."

"Ah, yes." said William, "but where will I find your body?"

"You will find me just a short ways up this little brook under a pile of old brush."

"Okay, Bill, I'll take care of it first thing in the morning."

The next morning, William found what was left of Bill Eagles's body, exactly where his ghost said it would be. Bill finally got his wish and was properly buried, and no one saw him again.

End of story? Not quite. Several years later in Springhill, Nova Scotia, a man by the name of Shacksteed, who lay on his deathbed, had something to get off his chest before words left him for good. He wanted more than anything to confess to those who were gathered around his deathbed that he had murdered Bill Eagles for his new boots.

William Scott confirmed that there had been no footwear near the skeletal remains of Bill Eagles.

Oh, a passing thought. Next time you folk up in Colchester County buy a new pair of boots, stay clear of the Westchester mountain. Who knows? Mr. Shacksteed's ghost may be lurking on that high place.

Chapter Four

Seeing Things

He Told Me Himself

Clary had been out fishing almost all day, and he decided it was time to pack it in and turn the boat homewards. As he started from the fishing grounds, he had a strange feeling that something ominous was happening at home. He went up on deck for some fresh air to clear his troubled mind. Poking his head up through the hatch, he was startled to see his father sitting on the stern of the boat, cutting bait. Clary knew then that something was wrong at home: While it was not unusual for his father to be on deck, this time it was quite a shock—his father had not come on this trip because he had been ill.

When Clary tied his vessel up at the wharf, his brother was waiting for him. "It's dad, isn't it?" said Clary.

"Yes. How did you know?" asked his brother.

Clary looked at his brother with tears in his eyes and said, "Believe it or not, he told me himself."

Quick Pulse

Weather permitting, a couple of times a week "John" would drive his car to a logging road about five miles from his home in Windsor. He'd park the car, get out, and jog along the deserted road. John said he preferred the isolation of the woods to the town.

One evening while he jogged, John was startled to see a woman and two children coming toward him. The woman was walking with a limp and leaning heavily on a cane. When the woman saw John, she stopped, lifted her cane, and pointed it menacingly at John. For his part, John felt something like an electric shock go through his body, paralysing him.

The old woman and the two children proceeded toward him, coming so close, said John, that if he had been able to move he would have been able to reach out and touch the child closest to him. Once they had passed, the paralysis left his body and he could move again. When he turned to see where the old woman and children were, they had vanished. John says he continues to jog the old logging road but with trepidation. He has never run into the trio again.

Seeing is Believing

While attending Sunday services, Mr. Morrison was startled to see a couple suddenly appear in the pew in front of him. *Where on earth did they come from*, he thought to himself. He didn't recall seeing them come in. The man was quite tall, with thick brown hair, and the woman seated next to him was also tall. Under her hat, her hair was jet black.

Since Mr. Morrison couldn't see their faces, he was unable to describe what they looked like, but he was certain that he'd never seen them around the village. He couldn't explain why, but he had the strangest feeling that they were from another time. They seemed to be out of place, and their clothes looked very strange, not at all the fashion of the times.

Suddenly, as if the man knew what Mr. Morrison was thinking, he turned around and stared with empty eyes. The man then turned to the woman and whispered something in her ear and they disappeared right before Mr. Morrison's eyes. Mr. Morrison prayed feverishly after that.

In Passing

*A*lfred Boutillier was a student at the time of this maritime mystery. One summer, he worked on a construction gang upgrading roads. One day during lunchtime he heard the faint clanging of cowbells: He looked toward the sound but couldn't see anything. The sound of the bells got louder and soon he saw a man leading a team of oxen. Alfred nudged the worker next to him and commented on how handsome the oxen were. Alfred's neighbour turned to him with a confused expression on his face. He suggested to Alfred that he get out of the sun: He apparently saw nothing coming down that road but dust and black flies.

Alfred knew his fellow worker wasn't a man to kid around, so he said no more and turned his attention back to the team of oxen that were now abreast of him. As the team passed, the driver tipped his cap at Alfred and moved on. Alfred watched the team of oxen pass. They did not saunter off down the road, but vanished in front of his eyes. Oddly enough, however, Alfred could still hear the fading sound of the bells.

Ghost Wagon

*N*eil drove the big rigs, hauling fish to Boston. On one of his trips back home he passed through a small community typical in rural Maine. At one o'clock in the morning, Neil was starting to feel the long hours on the road. Suddenly out of nowhere appeared a horse and wagon, piled high with furniture. A man and woman were seated up front and three small children peered out between a table and chairs.

Neil knew that there was no way he could stop his rig in time. He said a silent prayer as the eighteen-wheeler slammed into the horse and wagon. When he got the rig stopped, he ran back to attend to the family. There was no sign of the horse and wagon. No wreckage, no bodies—nothing. Neil shook his head and drove quickly to the nearest hotel, where he spent a restless night, dreaming again and again of the ghost wagon.

The Glimmer Ghost

A favourite spot of Mike Salkin and his dogs was Horse Shoe Island Park. The Island is located in the west end of Halifax off Quinpool Road, a dozen giant steps from the Armdale Rotary. On a cold November night four years ago, Mike took the dogs for their nightly walk.

Tag-along saw it. So did Keeper and Prince. And Mike Salkin saw it too. What they all saw was the Glimmer ghost. Mike and his dogs were walking south facing the Dingle Tower when they first saw the ghost. It was up on a small peninsula, walking toward the water. It stopped Mike in his tracks when he realized it wasn't another person out for a late-night stroll.

"I realized," said Mike, "that all I could see was half of a body, from the waist down. There was ample light and nothing was obstructing my view."

So he wasn't seeing things. And without giving it a second thought, Mike, with the dogs in tow, headed toward the peninsula for a better look. Mike said he never took his eyes off whatever it was, but when he walked out on the peninsula, it was gone.

"There was no way it could have backtracked or jumped into the water without me hearing a splash…unless it was a ghost."

Mike later learned that over the years there have been several serious automobile accidents, even fatal ones, at the entrance to Horseshoe Island. Perhaps what Mike and his dogs witnessed was the ghost of one of those accident victims.

The dogs are gone to their spirit world, but eighty-four-year-old Mike Salkin is still active. During his evening walks he's drawn to Horseshoe Island, and onto that little peninsula, by some unknown power. Mike stands there waiting, looking, but since that first encounter with the Glimmer ghost, no shadowy figures have appeared…not yet, anyway.

Man's Best Friend… In Life and Death

The dog was very old and going blind. The vet said it was time to let Brandy go and suggested it would be best to put her to sleep. Reluctantly, Claire and David MacNeil agreed and their once beautiful Irish wolfhound, who had given them years of devotion, was put to sleep. The MacNeils never did get another dog. In time though, they had a beautiful daughter, who they named Grace.

The parents became concerned when, on more than one occasion, Grace, now three, spoke of seeing a large black dog sitting under the apple tree in their yard, looking up at her bedroom window. Where most children have an imaginary friend, Grace seemed to have an imaginary pet.

"What did this doggie look like?" asked her father. "Oh," said little Grace, "He's very big, with black fur." The MacNeils looked at each other with concern. The same thought passed through both their minds, but they shook their heads and shrugged it off. Grace had seen pictures of Brandy. That was probably it.

Later on that year, a huge fire broke out in the MacNeil home and spread quickly throughout the house. David MacNeil tried desperately to reach little Grace's bedroom, but the flames drove him back and the debris created a barricade through which he could not pass. The fire trucks arrived, but too late to save the home. The flames and smoke were overwhelming, even for the firemen, and it looked as if there was no hope for poor little Grace.

Clair and David were watching the flames engulf their house in despair, when, from the rear of the house, a fireman emerged carrying something. With a grin on his face he said to Claire and David, "Look what I found sitting under the apple tree in the backyard, out of harm's reach." In his arms was Grace.

"It's a miracle!" Claire exclaimed, crying and hugging her daughter.

"I don't know how it happened" said the fireman. "She was just sitting there safe and sound. Oh, and your dog is safe too. Nice big, black dog was sitting right next to her."

Watch Your !?*©=!% Tongue

Laurent J. D'Entremont of Lower West Pubnico, Nova Scotia, brought this little fish tale to my attention. Laurent remembers the subject of the story, an old man in question who drove around Pubnico in the early 1950s in a 1927 Model T Ford. Laurent was a mere kid at the time but he remembers Willie LeBlanc clearly.

The story goes like this: Early one morning Willie took his boat out to check his mackerel nets. They were empty most of the time, and that upset him to no end. He was a hot-tempered individual, and on his way back from the fishing grounds, he was swearing a blue streak because he had only caught three mackerel that day. As he sailed past the Baptist church, he let out a volley of curses, blaming the church for his bad luck. He then picked up the three mackerel and hurled them one by one at the church.

When he turned around, much to his horror, there was a stranger seated in the bow of the boat watching him! Willie was so scared that he would never even describe what the stranger looked like. Word has it he never swore again.

Chapter five

Unfinished Business

The Suit

*H*ere's one that'll knock your socks off.

Back in the thirties there was a Fredericton family of humble means that from time to time received hand-me-downs from fancy relatives in the United States. One day a large box of clothes arrived, including a brand new blue pinstripe suit. A letter from their cousin Minnie pinned to the suit lapel explained that her brother, their recently deceased cousin Charles, had owned the suit. Charles had wanted to be buried in the suit, but the family was a frugal lot and decided it would be an awful waste of a brand-new suit. So they sent the suit to cousin Angus, as they knew it would fit him beautifully. They were sure Charles wouldn't have minded a bit.

Angus was thrilled at his expensive new suit and hurried up to his bedroom to try it on. Funny thing, though, it was as if the suit had a mind of its own. Angus had to struggle to get it on. Every time he'd lift his foot to pull a pant leg on, he'd fall over, like someone was pushing him off-balance. Finally, he got the suit on. When Angus came downstairs, everyone told him how grand he looked.

At church that Sunday the neighbours noticed the new suit and told Angus how spiffy he looked. Angus felt good. Halfway through the service, though, he felt something pulling on his suit collar. He turned around thinking someone might be teasing him, but the people in the pew behind him were watching the priest piously. Then something was pulling at Angus's waist. When he looked down he saw his three-button suit jacket being undone, as if with invisible hands. And something was pulling his suit jacket off his shoulders! Angus fled from the church, and by the time he got home all he was wearing was his Stanfields.

It seemed Cousin Charles did mind, after all.

Annie's Brooch

This sad ghost tale takes place in Liverpool, Nova Scotia. The account my storyteller gave differs slightly from the tale as it's told by "Ted" R. Hennigar in his book *Scotian Spooks, Mystery and Violence*.

Willie and Annie grew up together knowing that one day they would get married. But first, Willie needed to save up some money for a house for them to live in. Though he hated the thought of leaving his Annie, and he worried that some handsome young man may come along and court and marry her, Willie was determined: he decided to head to Boston to make his way.

The streets of Boston were not paved with gold and Willie found it hard to save for the home he planned to build back home for Annie. Meanwhile, Annie saved what she could from her job at a local Liverpool store for their life together. The young lovers wrote to each other regularly, dreaming of their reunion. When he was not working, Willie would walk the streets of Boston looking in all the shop windows. One day, he happened upon a beautiful gold brooch in the shape of a rose with a diamond in the centre. He wanted it for Annie more than anything in the world, but he knew he shouldn't spend any of the money he was saving for their home. Ever determined, Willie managed to save enough money working a part-time evening job to buy the brooch. He sent it home to Annie with all his love. When Annie received the gift she wrote and told Willie she would treasure it always.

Willie worked in Boston for three more years until finally he had saved enough money to return to Liverpool, marry Annie, and build their dream home on the outskirts of town.

Willie and Annie loved children, but sadly they were unable to have any of their own. Willie's six year-old niece, Martha, spent a lot of time at their place, becoming almost like a daughter to them.

One day, Annie discovered her brooch was missing. Annie thought Martha may have been playing with it, but when she and Willie questioned their niece, the girl denied playing with it.

The missing brooch caused an argument between Annie and Willie. He thought Annie had been irresponsible by leaving it someplace for Martha to find. Angry words passed between the two—the only serious argument they ever had. They never found the brooch, and it remained a quiet bone of contention, always there in the background during even their happiest times together.

Two years later, Martha died from a childhood illness. Willie and Annie missed her very much and often thought of her.

The years passed and Annie and Willie remained devoted to each other. Willie watched his love finally slip away and die of consumption. To honour her memory, he always kept a light on in the house and always set the table for the two of them. He visited her grave regularly and always kept a fresh supply of flowers in a wooden vase he made and placed on her grave. He was as devoted to her in death as he had been in life.

On the way home from the cemetery one day, Willie had an uneasy feeling. When he got home, he thought perhaps he was coming down with the flu and retired early. He lay in bed listening to the rain on the roof until he fell into a listless sleep. Some time during the night, Willie was awakened by a sound in the far corner of the room. He lit the lamp: there, looking back at him were Annie and little Martha, holding hands. The child looked upset, as though she had been scolded, and Annie looked white and pitiful. Her brown hair was wet and drops of water poured down her face. She stepped toward the bed and said, "Willie, we have found the brooch. Martha remembered where she left it. Come."

The ghosts of Annie and Martha started out into the hall toward the attic door. Grabbing the lamp, Willie followed. Annie opened the door and Martha went up first, then Annie and Willie after her. Martha walked toward a small hole in the floor. Willie remembered the hole from when he built the house—there wasn't enough lumber at the time so he left it as it was, an opening barely large enough for a child to climb through.

When Martha came to the opening, she got down on her knees and poked her head inside. She reappeared and passed Willie a small bundle of mesh cloth.

Willie set the lamp on the attic floor and unrolled the cloth—Annie's wedding veil—to reveal the beautiful brooch that Martha had hidden so many years before. He stared with disbelief at the long-lost brooch. With tears in his eyes, Willie turned to his wife and niece, but they had disappeared. He returned to his room and placed the veil and brooch under his pillow.

Sleep came hard to Willie that night. A couple of days later, during another summer rainstorm, the ghost of Annie appeared to Willie. Annie stepped closer to Willie's bed, and again, he noticed her face and hair were soaked. Annie looked down at Willie and spoke: "We have the brooch back, Willie. Let's not quarrel any more. Please, come help me."

Willie reached for her, but she backed toward the door and beckoned him to follow. "Come help me, Willie. I am so cold and wet."

Willie dressed quickly and followed the ghost of his wife out into the rain, toward the cemete ry. When they reached her grave, Willie looked down on the simple headstone and the flower vase he'd lovingly made for his dear Annie. When he looked up, her ghost was gone. Willie called her name repeatedly, but there was no response. She had left him alone again.

Summer was drawing to a close, and the weather turned cold and rainy. Once again Annie appeared to Willie, soaked to the skin. Her beautiful brown hair was hanging limp over her shoulders. She begged Willie to help her and back to the cemetery they went. As before, when Annie got to her grave, she vanished.

Willie woke early the next morning and headed for the cemetery. He brought a few pink chrysanthemums with him, deciding it was about time he replaced the peonies which had been there since early summer. As he picked up the vase, he noticed the bottom had rotted out, leaving a large hole under the vase which had been there since early summer. He picked up a stick and poked. It was then that he realized what had been bothering Annie. Each time she appeared, she was drenched, and she always came during a rainstorm. She had been trying to tell Willie that water was pouring down on her face through the hole in the grave. Even though he realized fixing the hole would mean never seeing Annie again, he did what he had done for her in life—made her happy. He fixed the hole…and never looked on his beloved again.

Row, Row, Row Your Ghost

*I*n the last century, boating was a popular pastime, and boats were available to rent by the hour, the day, or the week on Nova Scotia's Eastern Shore. One afternoon, a Mr. Hampton showed up at the boathouse wanting to rent a rowboat to take to an island he was interested in buying. The rental shop owner told Mr. Hampton he had only one boat left, and that, well, it was haunted. Mr. Hampton smiled and said that whoever was haunting the boat could join him for the ride.

Halfway across the lake, the man began to have some difficulty keeping the boat on course. It seemed to have a mind of its own and kept veering off toward the middle of the lake. Suddenly the boat dipped to one side and there was a loud splash, as if someone had jumped over the side. Mr. Hampton could hear gasping and thrashing in the water, but no one was there. After a few minutes, the splashing sounds stopped. When he got to the island and pulled the boat up on the beach, Mr. Hampton noticed a puddle of water on one of the seats and the floor of the boat, but couldn't think of how the water got there.

His return trip was without incident, and when he got back to the wharf he told the owner what had happened. The owner said, "I told you the boat was haunted. A man rented it last summer to go fishing. Somehow he lost his balance, fell overboard and drowned. Or maybe he jumped over. No one will ever know."

Broken Promises

This story takes place in Deer Island, New Brunswick. My contacts on Deer Island for this story are life-long residents Dale and Glenna Barteau.

In the mid-1850s, a resident of the town, John Hooper, was fed up with life and decided to end it all. According to reports, he was a little touched up top. He did have one child, a daughter who got off the island and headed for the States. Since no one heard from her since she left, one assumes she bought a one-way ticket.

Now, John Hooper had tried suicide once before, but failed. This time he made sure he would not. He tied a large bolder to his ankle, held the bolder in his arms and jumped into the pond behind his home.

John's relatives knew he didn't want a marker of any kind—he had stated as much many times before. He simply wanted to be buried in an unmarked grave, but when it comes to the wishes of the dead, the living think they know better. Big mistake on their part!

With good intentions, his family buried John Hooper in the field behind his house next to the very pond where had ended his life. Here, they erected a large tombstone to commemorate him. In life, he had stated time and time again this was the last thing he wanted. In death he'd let them know just how upset he was.

Not long after he was buried, people passing by his grave noticed the tombstone lying on the ground a few feet from his grave. Naturally, they reported it to his relatives. His relatives, in turn, had workmen put it back, this time more securely. All of this to no avail. Every time workmen put the stone back, it would end up a few feet from the grave, lying on its side.

Stories began circulating that old John Hooper's ghost was upright and restless. It became so upsetting to island residents that soon they avoided the area altogether.

Meanwhile the family, as feisty and stubborn as John himself, thought they would fix crazy old John for good. They decided to put something there that could not be moved or pushed over. They had the workmen lay a concrete slab first, and then set the marker in it. When family members went to check days later, they found the tombstone split in half with one section lying flat on the ground.

As far I know, John Hooper's ghost hasn't been seen around lately. As I understand it, there is a small and simple stone marking his grave. He finally got his way after all.

Let this to be a lesson. It's wise to respect the wishes of someone who has gone over to the other side. If you don't, the power of the deceased may come back and haunt the you-know-what out of you.

The Mystery of the Grey Lady

There are many versions of encounters people claim to have had with the mysterious Grey Lady. My own research places the Grey

Lady in Seaforth, for two very good reasons: Firstly, the south shore version has always appeared to be the most authentic account to me. And secondly, Dr. Helen Creighton places the Grey Lady in Seaforth as well, in her book *The Folklore of Lunenburg County.*

The facts were told to Professor Carmen Stone, of the University of Kings College in Halifax, and her mother by Reverend Robert Norwood, the son of Reverend Joseph Norwood, who had several encounters with the Grey Lady.

Sometimes ghosts attach their spirits to one person. In this 1931 story, the Grey Lady's attachment was to Reverend Joseph Norwood, the rector of the Anglican church of New Ross, and she wouldn't let go. She appeared everywhere, disturbing him so profoundly that the good reverend asked to be transferred to another parish. He got his wish, and was posted to Seaforth. Of course, that didn't end his problems with the Grey Lady. No sooner was he in his new surroundings than—lo and behold—the Grey Lady appeared on the landing of the rectory. In frustration, Reverend Norwood spoke to the apparition. He made the sign of the cross and said, "In the name of the Father and the Son and the Holy Ghost, speak." And what was the Grey Lady's reply? She looked the good priest in the eye, and told him that a great wrong had been done in which she had played a part. She instructed Reverend Norwood to go to a certain house on Morris Street in Halifax and deliver a message.

Reverend Norwood went to the Morris Street address the very next day, and discovered it was the home of the ghost's sister. To make absolutely sure there was a relationship between the two, he asked to see a family album. He turned over the pages until he came to a picture of the apparition he had seen and he said, "This is her." He then delivered the Grey Lady's message.

The Grey Lady wanted to tell her sister where an important document was hidden, and ask for forgiveness over a quarrel they'd had. The sister said she had forgiven her a long, long time ago and was thrilled to receive the information about the document. For his part in this, the reverend was never bothered by the Grey Lady again.

Irma Gets Even

*M*ary Kate waved goodbye to her children and stood watching in the doorway until they were safely on the school bus. Returning to the kitchen, she poured a cup of coffee and sat at the table, enjoying the peace and quiet. She thought of her husband, who was out of town on business but would be home by the weekend.

Suddenly, out of the corner of her eye, Mary Kate saw something move. She froze. Slowly, she turned her head toward the stove. Drawing a sharp intake of breath, Mary Kate stepped back. Right beside the stove, a blurry form was slowly taking shape. As the apparition became clearer Mary Kate could see what appeared to be a tall, thin woman in her late fifties. There was some grey in her hair, but it was mostly black, and she wore it high in a bun. She was wearing a black dress with a white collar. Mary Kate shook her head. *It has to be my imagination*, she thought. *Either that or I need a new prescription for my glasses.*

Mary Kate stared at the form for a long time, transfixed. The apparition had her hand on a copper kettle on the woodstove. Mary Kate blinked and looked again at the stove. It was the woodstove that had been in the kitchen before Mary Kate and her husband had modernized everything. She recognized it from before the renovations. Mary Kate looked around. The kitchen and everything in it was from another time, as was the apparition.

The ghost was fading in and out, and Mary Kate could make out the sound of water boiling in the kettle.

She was torn between two options. Should she run like mad, or make contact with the spirit? She was surprised to note that she wasn't afraid. Her curiosity was getting the better of her, and she wondered how to address the ghost. Would the ghost acknowledge her?

Her dilemma was solved when the ghost slowly turned her head towards Mary Kate and spoke directly to her. "It was deliberate, you know. He pushed me. He shoved me down the stairs and my head hit the banister and that was it. He killed me to get me out of the way. The next thing I knew I had been waked with all those hypocrites pouring out their pack of lies. Of course, him being mayor at the time, there wasn't much of an investigation. Tripped and fell down the stairs was what he told the investigators, and they bought it, lock, stock and barrel. But I swore I'd get even with him. So, here I am!"

Mary Kate wanted to be as friendly as possible—the last thing she wanted to do was upset a ghost. So she smiled and said, "It was your husband then, who pushed you down the stairs?"

The apparition nodded. "Indeed, it was. I've waited all these years to catch up with him and finally get even with the old coot. People should know what he did. He shouldn't be allowed to get away with it. With your help he'll get what he deserves."

Mary Kate's eyes narrowed. "My help? Meaning what?"

"Well, as a spirit, I'm limited as to what I can do and where I can go. Ghosts have different abilities, as do humans. Unfortunately, I'm not the travelling kind of ghost. I can't go where I please. I'm stuck in this place. Can't leave the house by myself. But I can if I become part of you. Kind of piggybacking, you might say. I'll be invisible and you won't even know I'm there. Think of me as an extra sweater."

Mary Kate shook all over just thinking about it. "You want me to help you do away with your husband?"

"No, no, of course not. No violence of any kind. I just want to face him one more time before he dies, which I'm hoping won't be long. As a matter of fact, today is his one hundredth birthday. I'm sure there'll be a birthday party for him, and I'd like to be there."

"And where is he?"

"Oh, I've been keeping tabs on his whereabouts. I can still read the papers, you know. Sometimes even over your shoulder. He's in a nursing home. So…you'll help me then?"

Mary Kate raised her eyebrows at the ghost. "Do I have a choice?"

"Not really. I can cause some real problems if you decide otherwise. You know, move things around. Flood the bathroom. Scare the children. You want that?"

"No, of course not. Let's get on with it then. I'm Mary Kate and you are, I mean, you *were*…?"

"Irma."

"Well, Irma, when do you want to go?"

"This afternoon. I want to get to him before he up and dies on me."

Mary Kate agreed, and Irma disappeared, stating she'd be back in the afternoon. In her absence, Mary Kate made a few phone calls and found what she was looking for. A friend at the local newspaper read the story to her. Irma had been telling the truth: "*Fall Kills Mayors' Wife. Foul Play Not Suspected,*" read the front-page headline from forty years ago.

It was about ten past three when Mary Kate drove into the nursing home parking lot. She quickly crossed the parking lot to the main entrance and went inside. She scanned the lobby until she found the ladies' room. Following Irma's instructions, she walked briskly towards it and went inside. As soon as she was inside, Irma's ghost stepped away from Mary Kate.

The apparition told Mary Kate to stay in the ladies' room until she returned. "Once I leave here," she told Mary Kate, " I'll be invisible and only my husband will see me." Then, Irma disappeared.

A sign with bold red letters above the solarium door wished Seth a happy one-hundredth birthday. Irma stepped inside. There were several residents seated around the brightly lit room. At one end, some of the residents were playing cards, other were watching television. There was chatter and laughter coming from the other end of the room, and Irma moved toward the sound, floating across the room and coming to stand behind a woman. Irma stole a look around. He was sitting in a wheelchair, grinning from ear to ear. Irma had to admit that he looked pretty good for a hundred.

All heads turned when a young woman carrying a birthday cake followed by a group of nurses came into the room singing "Happy Birthday." Those gathered around Seth moved away to make room for the birthday revellers. Irma stepped right in front of the table where the birthday cake was placed. The cake had ten lit candles. One candle for each decade, Irma supposed. A heavy-set woman who appeared to be in charge suggested Seth blow out the candles and make a wish. "Take a deep breath now," she told him. He did…and it turned out to be the last one he ever took. As Seth was taking the breath, Irma suddenly appeared behind the cake. She bent down so only her face showed between the flickering lights of the candles. It was only seconds, but Irma saw the look of disbelief on Seth's face.

Once they were back in the car, Mary Kate asked Irma if everything had gone as planned.

"Oh, yes, yes indeed," she replied. "The old coot got the biggest birthday surprise of his life."

When they got back to Mary Kate's house, Irma told Mary Kate that there was no need or reason for her to stay any longer. With that, Irma's ghost was gone.

The following morning, Mary Kate again stood in the doorway until the children were safely on the school bus. She went into the kitchen, poured herself a cup of coffee, and picked up the morning newspaper. When she opened it, she noticed an article in the corner right away: "*Former mayor dies suddenly during his 100th birthday party.*" Mary Kate couldn't help but smile when she read the concluding line: "An employee of the nursing home observed, 'It was as if he had seen a ghost.'"

The History Lesson

Grade four teacher Miss Goss stood at the window watching her students enjoy recess, at a school in Sydney Mines, Cape Breton, in the early 1940s. She noticed a lone child standing on the sidelines, watching. Miss Goss noticed something else highly unusual: The child was dressed head to toe in very odd clothing. The style was outdated, as though from another century.

Miss Goss decided to find out who the little girl was and why she was dressed that way. She made her way through the schoolyard, but by the time she reached the other side of the playground, the child was gone. Miss Goss asked the children where the little girl had gone, but they didn't seem to know who their teacher was talking about. The bell rang and the children filed inside.

Miss Goss instructed the children to read their favourite stories. All was quiet in the classroom. The teacher, too, was intent on her reading until a movement in the back of the class caught her attention. When she looked up, the same little girl in old-fashioned dress stood in the back of the classroom, staring at her. There was something strange about the child. It was as if she was in some kind of trance. The children, Miss Goss noticed, were not aware of the girl's presence. Was she the only one who could see her? What should she do? She decided to confront the student, but when she looked up again the child was gone.

Miss Goss had to shake her head because what happened next was beyond belief: An invisible hand was writing a message on the blackboard. The letters slowly came together. They formed two simple and terrifying words. "FIND ME!"

The teacher turned and looked at the students but all heads were buried in their books. "Excuse me class," she said. "Can you see what has been written on the blackboard?" Puzzled, the children shook their heads. One student replied with a smirk, "Are you seeing things, Miss Goss? There isn't anything written on the board." The teacher was now truly perplexed and responded, "No. I just wanted to see if you were paying attention, that's all." Just then the bell rang and with a sigh of relief, she dismissed the class with a reminder not to forget their homework.

When the students left, Miss Goss pondered the meaning of the message on the blackboard. Did it mean the student was somewhere in the building? If so, where? Should she alert the school authorities? But how could she possibly tell them that she had seen a ghost—and that she was the only one?

Miss Goss was getting ready to leave when the door opened and an elderly man came into the room. He was wearing coveralls and carrying a trash basket. "Sorry miss, I thought everyone was gone." Miss Goss studied the man. "I haven't seen you around here before."

"Oh, you're right. I'm what you'd call a part-timer. My name's Thibodeau. Henry Thibodeau. Worked here full time for more than fifty years."

Miss Goss wondered if this man knew something about the mysterious child. "Tell me, Mr. Thibodeau, did something tragic occur in this school at any time?"

"Let me see…well, at one time, this was a small one-room school—pretty as a picture—until it was replaced with this school. Built right over the very spot where the one roomer was. As the story goes, one day a student by the name of Amy McCue and an itinerant maintenance worker vanished. According to Amy's teacher, the girl had been sent down to the basement to get some school supplies. Unfortunately, the teacher forgot about her until nearly two hours later. When she went down to see what was keeping the girl, she was nowhere to be found. She was never found, actually. But many years later we found out what happened to the missing maintenance worker. He was drowned while fishing on George's bank."

Miss Goss's interest was piqued. "What do you think happened to the little girl?"

Mr. Thibodeau was becoming agitated. "Some folks around here say she was murdered. I would tend to agree," he replied. Miss Goss sensed he would not talk further about the issue. Hurriedly, she thanked him and left.

Late that night Miss Goss bolted upright in bed. She had been having a terribly weird dream. Mr. Thibodeau was in it, showing her a sketch of something on a piece of paper. Miss Goss remembered him pointing at one specific spot. "She's there. Find her," he repeated. A voice told the frightened woman to go to the school immediately. She got out of bed, dressed quickly, grabbed a flashlight and hurried to the school.

She had to hold her right hand with her left to keep it from shaking while she got the key into the back door lock. Once inside, she went directly to the basement. She found the narrow door that Mr. Thibodeau had pointed to over and over—it led to the room where he said the body of Amy McCue was buried. Miss Goss opened the door and shone her flashlight in. The room was small and empty. Hanging from the ceiling was a thin wire with a broken light bulb hanging from its socket. Cobwebs were everywhere. She shook when she thought of something crawling along the dirt floor. "Please god," she whispered, "No rats." There were small chunks of coal strewn over the dirt floor and she could hear a crunching sound when she stepped on them. She supposed the room had been the coal cellar one time, a theory confirmed when she found a small shovel. Positioning the flashlight on the floor so the light would fill most of the small space,

Miss Goss began digging. She worked for ten minutes, then stopped. There was no need to dig further. Miss Goss backed away. It was the same face she had seen in the schoolyard and classroom. She steeled herself to look at the body of Amy McCue. There was no decomposition whatsoever. It was as if she were simply asleep.

It was three o'clock in the morning; the teacher decided to stay until the school authorities arrived. No longer afraid, she moved to the far corner of the room and sat down. She brought her knees up close to her chest, wrapped her arms around her legs, put her head down on her knees, closed her eyes and waited for daylight.

That's where they found her the next morning. She told the authorities that she had seen the girl in the schoolyard and her classroom. She told them about the message that appeared on the blackboard. She also told of her meeting with the part-time janitor, the dream, and her gruesome discovery. When she mentioned Mr. Thibodeau's name, there was a stir and whispering. They asked her to describe Mr. Thibodeau and Miss Goss obliged. "He was quite tall. Over six feet I'd say. Black hair. A moustache. There was a tattoo on his left arm. I believe it was the fleur-de-lis." No one spoke for the longest time. They were all staring at Miss Goss.

The principal finally spoke: "The maintenance worker who went missing and was believed to be Amy's killer was Henry Thibodeau."

Rearview Mirror

*F*ranklin, who lived in Yarmouth, Nova Scotia, didn't know the used car he bought had been in an accident. Although the car wasn't that badly damaged, its owner, a woman in her late seventies, was killed. The coroner said she died of a severe blow to the head. The coroner was right, but the blow to the woman's head wasn't caused by the accident. Her impatient nephew, who couldn't wait for his inheritance, had dealt the deadly blow.

During the inquest, the nephew testified that he had been dozing off when suddenly the car spun out of control. He survived with only minor scratches but his poor, dear aunt was killed.

Franklin was unaware of this history when he bought the car. But every time he was in it, the hair on his neck stood ramrod straight and his body shook from an unknown fear. He was certain something supernatural was in the car with him.

One day, terror overwhelmed Franklin when he felt fingers squeezing his right shoulder. He looked down at his shoulder, but of course he couldn't see the hand that was touching him, so he pulled over to the side of the road, stopped the car and got out. He stepped to the rear window and peered inside. The back seat was empty.

Franklin got back into his car and drove to the dealership where he had bought it only a week before. He told the salesman the car was haunted. The salesman thought him strange, but listened anyway. When Franklin was finished telling the salesman what had happened, there was a long pause. Finally, the salesman said, "You're telling me we sold you a ghost car? Is that what you're saying?"

"Yes, that's what I'm saying. The car is haunted." The salesman slowly walked around the car, shading his eyes when he peeked through the windows. "Next," said the salesman, "you'll be telling me that the so-called ghost in the car is the little old lady that was killed."

"Killed?" said Franklin. "What are you talking about?"

The salesmen then told Franklin about the car accident. "But it didn't damage the car, really, or we would have told you about it."

Franklin was shocked to hear of the accident, and felt that the woman who had died must be trying to communicate with him for a reason. The thought of getting back into that car made him feel queasy. "Look, I'm not interested in driving that car anymore. Can we do an exchange?"

The salesman shook his head. "Mister, no way. If there was something mechanically wrong, we'd take care of it, but a ghost? No, I think not."

Franklin also shook his head as, despite his foreboding, he got back in the car and drove off. On the way back to the city the feeling that he wasn't alone came over him again. When he glanced in the rearview mirror his breath caught somewhere in his chest and he felt like he was going to pass out. He pulled over to the shoulder and stopped and waited until his breathing became somewhat normal again.

In the mirror, staring back at him, he saw a frail old woman. Franklin noticed she had a nasty bump on her forehead. He didn't know exactly what to do so he decided the best thing was to get out of the car. But before he could open the door, she stopped him. "Please, you must help me. I'm a prisoner of this car. It was my nephew who killed me, not the accident. He did it for the money but he can't have it. Will you help me? My nephew struck me with a hammer and then hid it in the stump of an rotting tree. It's only a few miles from here. Drive there and I'll show you. Then you can call the police."

Franklin felt dizzy. "And what do I tell them? I got the information from the victim? Is that what I tell them?"

"You don't have to tell them anything more than where the hammer is hidden and who did it," replied the old woman, with desperation in her eyes.

Franklin's sympathy for the woman overcame his fear, and he decided to help her. "Alright, alright, I'll do it," he said. "But then, you'll have to leave my car. Deal?"

"Deal," the old woman agreed.

Following the woman's directions, it didn't take Franklin long to find the hammer in the woods. He was careful not to touch it, and used a pair of gloves to lift the bloodstained weapon from the tree trunk. He carefully placed the hammer in plain view, and, upon returning to the car, dialed the police on his cell phone. "Done," he said as he got back into the car. He looked in the back seat, but the old woman had already disappeared.

Cold Case Files

I credit the *Sackville Tribune-Post* for the following story, which appeared in The *Daily Gleaner* under the headline: "Fredericton couple found shot to death."

It was Tuesday, October 19, 1965, at suppertime for most. John and Isabelle Felsing, and their dog, Heather, were walking along the peaceful Oromocto Flats outside Fredericton, New Brunswick. Suddenly, gun shots shattered the silence and the Felsings fell to the ground, mortally wounded. The murderous shots were fired from a 12-gauge shotgun.

Was the shooting deliberate? Or was it the action of a careless hunter?

Heather, the Felsings' dog, was nervous but protective. She stayed by her owners until 10:30 that night, when the bodies were illuminated by taxi headlights and consequently discovered. When the Mounties arrived, Heather wouldn't let them near the bodies, and an animal handler from the SPCA had to be brought in to remove the frightened dog.

Following the shootings, speculation about whether the deaths were deliberate or accidental began spreading throughout the community. Mr. Felsing had been a buyer in a government purchasing department, and according to rumour, he was killed to stop him from releasing damaging information against other officials. No one could provide facts to back up these accusations, however. Following an intensive investigation, the RCMP concluded that a careless duck hunter accidentally shot the Felsings, but the file remains open.

Here's something to ponder. According to journalist and author Dorothy Dearborn, of Hampton, New Brunswick, a police official not with the RCMP came to her with more information. He told her that an elderly hunter included in his will a confession that he accidentally shot the Felsings. As of this writing, the Fredericton detachment of the RCMP has no knowledge of any such confession.

My thanks to Genevieve Kilburn and Stephanie Lutz of the Harriet Irving Library, University of New Brunswick, for assistance in obtaining many of the facts and dates for this mystery.

The Ghost in the Tin Lizzie

*M*r. Forester considered himself very fortunate indeed to have been in the right place at the right time. He had placed an ad in the local newspaper looking for a small, out-of-the-way place on the water in the St. Margaret's Bay area, and immediately received a call from someone willing to sell to him. Mrs. Mueller's place sounded like it was exactly what he wanted. He knew as soon as he saw it that it was perfect. It was a typical English-style cottage, set back from the main road, with century-old oaks on either side of the small lane it was on, Ocean View Drive.

When Mr. Forester got out of the car Mrs. Mueller was waiting for him on the stoop. He was surprised at how old she was—on the telephone she had sounded quite young. She had long white hair and she came toward him smiling, with her hand outstretched. Mr. Forester could not help but notice how long and twisted her fingers were, and how cold they felt when he shook her hand. He figured it was poor circulation from old age.

"You're the perfect person to own my beloved cottage," Mrs. Mueller said, smiling. "I can always tell an honest person by their voice." She beamed at him.

Mrs. Mueller showed him all around the property. It was, without question, perfect. Absolutely what he had hoped for. There were three bedrooms, a dining room and a large living room that faced the ocean. Standing in front of the picture window, Mr. Forester admired the view. The land sloped gradually down to the cliff's edge, and a well-worn path led down to the cliff, then ended abruptly. The drop, she told him, was 230 feet. She came and stood next to him. "The view from the top of the cliff is breathtaking," she said. "Shall we take a closer look?" Mr. Forester followed as Mrs. Mueller led the way through the kitchen and out the back door. Halfway down the path, Mr. Forester noticed a small barn almost completely concealed by the overhanging branches of white pines.

"There's the barn. My late husband kept his car in there. No matter what the weather, rain or shine, his precious car was kept inside."

Interested, Mr. Forester asked, "What kind of car was it?"

"*Is* Mr. Forester. It *is* a 1927 Model T, affectionately known as a Tin Lizzie."

Mr. Forester's face lit up. "You mean it's in there now?"

"Yes, Mr. Forester. Would you like to see it?"

"Would I! Of course I would. If I may say, Mrs. Mueller, I'm somewhat of an afficionado."

When Mrs. Mueller opened the garage door, Mr. Forester couldn't believe what he was looking at. The Model T was still in showroom condition.

"I can't believe it, Mrs. Mueller. I just don't know how it can still be in such pristine condition after all these years parked in this barn."

"Perhaps," said Mrs. Mueller, "my husband's spirit?"

Mr. Forester nodded and smiled.

"Go ahead and sit in it, Mr. Forester."

"You don't mind?"

"Of course not. I insist."

Mrs. Mueller then moved to the other side and got in. She patted the driver's seat, smiling.

Mr. Forester got behind the wheel. Not only was it in showroom condition, but it also had that special new-car smell. Maybe he could buy this from her as well!

"Go ahead," Mrs. Mueller said, "Go ahead take hold of the wheel."

Just as soon as Mr. Forester's fingers wrapped around the wheel the engine turned over.

Startled, Mr. Forester tried to pull his hands off the wheel, but no matter how hard he tried, he couldn't remove them. The vehicle backed itself out of the garage and began to pick up speed as it moved toward the cliff. Mr. Forester tried to steer away from the cliff, but it was as if someone else was steering. He tried desperately to jump out of the hurtling car, but he couldn't. Something kept him anchored to his seat. When Mr. Forester turned to Mrs. Mueller the wind was blowing her long white hair around and over her head, making her look for all the world like a cackling witch. Mr. Forester screamed as the Tin Lizzie went over the cliff into the void below.

The young man turned the car down Ocean View Drive. He turned to his pretty bride and said, "Keep your fingers crossed, honey—this could be our new home."

When the young man stopped the car an elderly woman with long white hair stood on the stoop smiling. She suggested they look around outside first. She led the way along the well-worn path toward the high cliffs. When they came to the open garage, the young man stopped in disbelief. "That's not a Tin Lizzie, is it?"

"Why, yes...yes, it is...Would you folks like to sit in it?"

Dead Ringer

*T*his is the second story passed on to me by Russell McManus of Truro, Nova Scotia.

One of Russell's hobbies is collecting coins. When the Truro Exhibition closed for the season, Russell grabbed his metal detector and headed to the field that was used as the parking lot. He began his search for coins near the horse barns. Luck was on his side: where usually he found only new coins, keys and nails, this time he discovered a few very old coins, along with some blackened nails and glass. And the ground nearby contained small pieces of old charred wood, indicating that there had been a building there at one time, and one which had possibly burned down.

Russell's metal detector was recording a signal about eight inches deep. He dug down, and just as he was going to pick up whatever his detector had found, two horses in a nearby coral went wild. The horses reared onto their hind legs, pawing at the air with their front hooves, clearly terrified of something. They were snorting, whinnying and trying to break out of the coral. Two handlers had to rush into the coral to calm them down. Russell, meanwhile, pulled an old horseshoe out of the hole he had dug. And as he lifted the horseshoe from its grave, he heard a horse thundering toward him at full gallop. Russell was frozen to the spot. He couldn't move a muscle, and could only keep his head down to protect himself. Something brushed past, knocking him off balance. When he got to his feet there was no sign of the charging horse—the two horses in the coral were calm and grazing.

I wonder if Russell McManus has that horseshoe nailed to anything, or if he did the wise thing and put it back where he found it.

'Some Monster of Iniquity'

There are three good reasons to enter a cemetery: to be buried, to visit a loved one's grave, or to read the many fascinating tombstone inscriptions you can often find. In the Methodist cemetery in Middle Sackville, New Brunswick, there's an inscription on a tombstone that reveals to the world that the man buried there did not die of natural causes. No, William Fawcett was murdered!

This is the inscription on Mr. Fawcett's tombstone:

In memory of William Fawcett who was a plain industrious hospitable and deeply pious man whose uniform and Christian conduct gained him the respect of all who became acquainted with him while reading one of Mr. Wesley's sermons.

His immortal spirit was instantly precipitated into the eternal world to take possession of its final rest by some monster of iniquity that will be discovered at the last day who intentionally shot him dead through the kitchen window on the evening of June 19, 1832 in the sixty-third year of his age.

The coroner reported that the body of Mr. Fawcett was found in a seated position, a book of John Wesley's sermons fixed firm in his hand. It lay open at Wesley's text on 2 Samuel 18:33, "O my son Absalom, my son, my son Absalom. Would I had died instead of you."

Here the plot thickens. The coroner's report concluded, "What renders this dispensation more particularly depressing, is that suspicion has fallen on his only son, Rufus, as perpetrator of the murder." Rufus was charged with the crime, but was then acquitted after a trial. He left for the United States and the murder of William Fawcett remains a mystery to this very.

Chapter Six

You Can't Outrun a Forerunner

Empty Saddle

*M*abel of Lower Sackville told me this story in a theatre line-up. She credits it to her grandfather. It was his great grandfather, Victor, who was involved in the tale.

Victor was driving his team of Morgans to town for supplies when the incident happened. Suddenly abreast of his wagon, there appeared a beautiful and magnificent white stallion. After he caught his breath, Victor noticed something most peculiar. Although there was no one in the saddle, someone or something was holding the reins taut. He also noticed the great brown eyes of the horse bulging out of their sockets and its flared nostrils. Victor knew horses better than most and he knew this one was afraid of something.

Victor's throat was so dry that when he spoke his voice cracked "Who is it? What do you want from me?" But as soon as he spoke, the horse disappeared. Victor tried to find out who owned a white stallion, but no one for miles around owned such a horse. A mystery to be sure.

Between the Holly

*I*t was a week before Christmas and preparations were in full swing at the MacDonald homestead. At the urging of his family, Dan R. headed into the woods to chop down the family Christmas tree.

That afternoon, under a clear and cold sky and with a newly sharpened axe slung over his broad shoulders, Dan R. headed into the deep forest. Most people who entered these woods didn't wander too far off the beaten path for fear of getting lost…or of what might be watching from the trees. But Dan R. knew the woods. They had been his playground as a boy.

After an hour of walking through the thick brush, he came into a clearing. Sitting atop a small knoll he spotted the perfect balsam fir. He placed the axe to one side and began clearing the snow from around the trunk. Suddenly a shadow crossed over him.

The fine hairs on his neck stood out and a shiver went through him. A bear was the first thing to cross Dan R.'s mind as he reached for the axe and turned around slowly. Seated on a horse-drawn sleigh and staring silently at Dan R. were a man, a woman and a child. The child was so bundled in winter clothing that Dan R. couldn't tell whether it was a boy or girl. The one thing he could see was the bright red Santa cap the child wore. Dan R. stood rooted to the spot, puzzled. There was no road to enable a sleigh to get this far into the woods, only a footpath. Yet here before his eyes was a horse and sleigh with three people in it. But how did it get there?

As a police officer, Dan R. was a cautious and intuitive man who never ignored the signals from within. He tightened his grip on the handle of the axe just in case. He smiled, nodded and spoke. "Hello there folks. Getting a tree for Christmas. You look like you're lost, are you?" When there was no response, Dan R. walked toward the sleigh. When he was close enough to see their faces, he noticed the child was weeping, as was the woman. The man wore a blank stare. Dan R. noticed something else was not right with the scene. Water was dripping from their clothes, the sleigh and the horse. It was as if they had just come through a torrential downpour.

As soon as he took another step, the horse, sleigh and family vanished before his eyes! The shock was so sudden that Dan R.'s legs came out from under him and he fell to the snow. When he recovered his senses, he decided it was time to get the tree and get out of there. An hour later Dan R. crossed over the logging road and made his way down the hill into his backyard. He was happy and relieved to see his home.

After supper, Dan R. and his wife watched the children decorate the tree. They sang Christmas carols and ate sweets. He was still dumbfounded by the afternoon's events but did not want to alarm his family or put a damper on the festivities, so he held his tongue.

When the kids were finally in bed, Dan R. told his wife what he had seen in the woods earlier in the day. "The people you described sound like the new folk who moved into the old MacGregor homestead. "Perhaps it was a forerunner," his wife said. Dan R. was not convinced by his wife's explanation, but exhausted from the days events, he fell asleep.

Dan R. was brought out of a deep sleep by an insistent knocking on the door. It was one his fellow officers, who stated he was needed at Moon Lake. There had been an accident. Someone had gone through the ice. Dan R. dressed hurriedly and made his way to the scene.

When Dan R. stepped out of his truck, an officer was waiting. He was holding a bright, red Santa cap in his hand. Dan R. knew then, without a doubt, that his wife was right—it had been a forerunner indeed.

The Coffin Maker

I was attending a memorial at a local funeral home when I heard this forerunner story. The incident happened over a hundred years ago in a small New Brunswick community near Riverview.

Murdock, the village undertaker and coffin maker, knew everyone for miles around. He was a sly old man who kept up on the state of the village, and always had just enough coffins at the ready. One night, the coffin maker was sound asleep when he was awakened by the sounds of someone sawing and hammering—and it sounded like it was coming from his workshop. Holding an oil lamp high, Murdock made his way downstairs through the kitchen and to the door that led to his workshop. When he unlocked the door and stepped inside, the shop was empty…except for the most beautiful coffin he had ever seen. It was an extra large one.

Murdock, smart man he was, knew a forerunner when he saw one. The village coffin maker and undertaker thought to himself, "just my size." He returned to bed and died peacefully in his sleep that same night.

A Knock on the Door

*H*ere's a story from Dr. Helen Creighton's popular *Bluenose Ghosts* book. Dr. Creighton loved the community of Pubnico and it is said she heard this story on one of her many visits to that area.

The story involves a girl from Halifax, and her brother, Willie, who at the time of this incident was serving in the army overseas.

One night there was a knock on the door. Even though it was late for visitors to be calling, the girl went downstairs to answer it. She was overjoyed when she opened the door to find Willie standing there, decked out in his uniform. In a sombre and sober voice he said to his sister, "My work is over. I've done what I had to do." The girl reached out to embrace her brother but as she did, he mysteriously disappeared.

Awakened by the knocking, the girl's father had come to investigate. When he saw his daughter standing in front of the empty door, he was angry with her. "What are you thinking opening the door to any stranger that might be there at three in the morning?" he said in a raised voice. Frightened and confused, she told her father, "Willie was just here. He stood right there on our front porch and said his work was done. I tried to hug him, but he just disappeared." Her father thought she must have been sleepwalking for how else could he explain why Willie would show up, make this statement, and then leave?

The next morning dawned clear and bright. Just as the girl and her father were sitting down to breakfast, there was a knock at the door. Hoping her brother had returned, the girl ran to the door to greet him. But Willie did not greet his sister at the door. Instead, a serviceman wished her good morning and handed her a telegram which began with those dreaded words "We regret to inform you…" Willie was dead.

All in the Family

*T*his ghost story involves three members of a family in Salsbury, New Brunswick: Lenore, Cordelia and John. Cordelia was well acquainted with ghosts and knew how to deal with them. She saw them all the time and, so we're told, even had conversations with some. She had this special talent, you know. Ghosts sought her out. They seemed to know that when they approached Cordelia she wouldn't scream or faint like some do. "Ghosts," Cordelia would say, "are everywhere. They pass through us on the street of our fair cities. Remember that cool breeze you felt on the hot August afternoon but there was no wind to speak of…?"

Case in point: One time while visiting her grandmother's grave at a Salsbury graveyard, Cordelia was seated on a bench when she observed a spirit wearing a military uniform looking at her. After many minutes had passed, he finally came over and sat next to her. The ghost asked Cordelia to get in touch with his family back in England and let them know what happened to him. She agreed to help but never did, of course. After all, he was a British soldier killed in the American Revolutionary War. Cordelia figured it was a bit too late to deliver that message!

Cordelia's brother, John, was of a different nature than his phantom-friendly sister. John's haunting began some fifty years ago when he bought an old farmhouse outside of Moncton, New Brunswick. He wasn't settled in for very long when he realized that something was terribly wrong in one room—the bedroom where he slept, as a matter of fact. It wasn't a place of welcome or rest, and he felt like an intruder in it. He was convinced the room was haunted. He never saw anything but he felt like he was being watched. His suspicions were confirmed when one night, while on his way upstairs to bed, he was suddenly lifted off his feet and shoved down the stairs by an invisible force.

Fed up and terrified, John made arrangements to fly to his sister's home in Florida. He needed to talk to Cordelia about what was in his bedroom and how to get rid of it. In the car on the way home from the airport, Cordelia said to her brother, "I invited you down, but you didn't have to bring the spirit with you." John was confused. "Spirit? I don't feel the spirit. How do you know it's here?"

"He's in the car with us now. He's been trying to drive the car off the road. Watch." Cordelia took her hands off the wheel and it suddenly spun to the left. She grabbed the wheel quickly to prevent the car from veering off the road.

John's visit to Florida was brief, and he returned to New Brunswick more tired and anxious than before. He had just arrived home when he received a call from Cordelia: "You didn't take the spirit back with you. It's still down here with me!" The ghost never did return to New Brunswick. I suppose it had something to do with the Florida weather.

Pressed by this writer, Lenore, the teller of these ghostly tales, confesses that from time to time she has premonitions. One Sunday afternoon, she told me, she was resting on her bed when suddenly a strange feeling came over her. She felt as though her body was suspended above the bed. Then a voice spoke to her. It said, "When your mother dies, you won't be able to get her coffin up the steps." Lenore immediately thought that this was silly because the steps were quite wide. Two years later Lenore and her family moved to another home and when her mother died, the undertaker told the grieving Lenore, "I'm sorry but I can't get the coffin up the steps: they're too narrow."

Lenore says seeing and talking to ghosts and having forerunners visit you is nothing new or strange. It's all in the family. True story.

Going Up?

*H*enry hurried across the lobby to the bank of elevators that would take him to the tenth floor of the hospital and to his mother's room. When the elevator door opened, Henry recognized the man standing in front of him as his neighbour, Mr. Harrington. This struck Henry as very strange, as his father had told him just that morning that Mr. Harrington was gravely ill and was in this very hospital, close to death. *He's obviously feeling better*, Henry thought to himself thankfully. Henry smiled and asked Mr. Harrington how he was feeling. Mr. Harrington didn't look at or answer Henry; he simply got off the elevator and started walking down the hallway. Henry watched his neighbour recede down the dimly lit hall. *Very strange*, Henry thought to himself, *very strange indeed*.

Following the visit with his mother, Henry stepped out into the corridor to discuss his mother's condition with his brother. At the other end of the corridor, the men noticed a commotion. Several people were coming out of a room embracing each other.

"Our neighbours, the Harrington family," Henry's brother told him.

"I forgot to tell you, their father passed away only a half hour ago." Henry stared at his brother. "That's not possible. I met Mr. Harrington on my way up not ten minutes ago."

"Oh, come on," said Henry's brother. "You must be mistaken. Mr. Harrington is in the room down the hall, dead."

Henry gave his brother a confused look. "No, no, I tell you. He was getting off the elevator. I spoke to him, but he kept on going without saying a word. Before the elevator door closed, I saw him leave the lobby. I'll never forget the look on his face—the god-awful look of man who was going someplace he didn't want to go."

Chains

*T*his ghostly tale takes place back in 1913. At that time, Levi Morrow was the keeper of the Wood Islands lighthouse. Like so many others, Levi became an innocent party to a forerunner's ghostly visit. He was awakened in the middle of the night by the sound of someone dragging chains. Not a good sound to hear at any time but especially during the dead of night.

Levi was drawn to the window. When he looked out he was shocked to see Captain Abraham Daley coming over the top of the shed that was attached to the lighthouse. Levi was startled nearly out of his wits. But Levi didn't hide under the blankets mumbling, "Go away, go away." No sir, not Levi. Instead he stood his ground and called out, "Is that you Abe?" There was no answer and no Captain Abraham Daley anywhere. So Levi went back to bed and probably spent the rest of the night staring into the darkness.

The following day, Captain Daley, who was retiring, was returning to Prince Edward Island on his final voyage. He had a full cargo onboard including a shipload of heavy chains. Near the mouth of Charlottetown harbour, the ship ran into trouble. The crew was saved, but not the good captain. Apparently as he toppled over the side, he got all tangled up in the chains and the weight took him to the bottom.

This forerunner came to me from the "Keepers of the light," Heather MacMillan of Wood Islands, PEI. Heather grew up on Maritime Mysteries at her father's knee. She credits the late Mrs. Abena Hume for this Maritime story. Levi Morrow was Abena's uncle.

And the Bell Tolls for Thee

*A*lso from Pubnico harkens this mystery of a bicycle's broken bell and what caused it to ring. Howard d'Entremont lives in a house that is over 150 years old. It belonged to his grandfather, Ludger d'Entremont, a fisherman.

Howard's story goes as such: Old Mrs. D'Entremont was hanging out the laundry in the backyard when she was startled to hear a faint ringing noise. It seemed to be emanating from their shed, so she crept closer to the shack to investigate. As she turned the corner, she was shocked to realize that the ringing was coming from Ludger's old bike—a bike whose bell had not worked in years!

It came to be known that, on the very same day, while towing another boat into the harbour, the cable snapped and hit Ludger d'Entremont on the head, sending him overboard to his death. The broken bell of the bicycle began ringing at the precise moment Ludger was killed.

Death Was His Companion

It was mid afternoon when I stopped at the Bras d'Or look-off on Route Four. Seated at a picnic table were three couples enjoying the scenery and a snack. I was invited to join them and it wasn't long before they wanted to know if I was writing another Maritime Mystery book, to which I replied "Yes. Hopefully, it will be out sometime in soon."

"Do you believe in forerunners, Bill?" asked of the picnickers.

"Of course," I replied. "Remember, I grew up in Cape Breton." Naturally, I asked why.

"Well," said the elderly gentleman, "I'll give you a piece of advice. Never try to outrun a forerunner. My friend Murdoch tried and died of a heart attack." Now I was intrigued and wanted to hear more. I wanted to know exactly what happened to his friend.

"Death was his companion that evening," said my storyteller. "It was a warm evening and my friend Murdoch decided to walk home from the office. He felt he needed to unwind, and was certain the walk would do him good. Halfway home he heard footsteps behind him. They were faint and distant at first but were steadily catching up with him. When he turned around to see who it was, there was no one there. He thought this was very strange indeed. Murdoch kept on. No sooner was he in full-stride than he heard the footsteps again. But this time they were much closer.

"Murdoch did what few people would ever think of doing. He spoke to whatever was following him. He knew it was of some supernatural force. 'Is it me you want?' he asked. 'Is that why you're following me, or is it some member of my family?' There was no reply because death is always silent.

"Murdoch then had a thought. If he could outrun the forerunner he'd be safe. So he ran for home as fast as he could. But no matter how fast he ran, the footsteps kept pace. When he reached the steps of his home, Murdoch collapsed. That's where his family found him lying in a heap muttering about death, footsteps and forerunners.

"The doctor said Murdoch was under a lot of stress and needed complete bed rest."

My storyteller shook his head and went on. "Poor Murdoch never had a chance to get well. Just before drifting off, he heard three knocks on his bedroom wall and he barely had time to turn his head toward the knocking when life left his body. The forerunner had caught up with old Murdoch in the end. Death always does."